The Case
of the
Missing Six

DIANNE GLASER

The Case
of the
Missing Six

DRAWINGS BY DAVID K. STONE

Holiday House · New York

J
G

Library of Congress Cataloging in Publication Data

Glaser, Dianne.
    The case of the missing six.

    SUMMARY: Two rambunctious boys spend their spring
vacation trying to trace several neighborhood pets that
have disappeared.
    [1. Mystery and detective stories] I. Stone,
David K. II. Title.
PZ7.G48045Cas   [Fic]   77-16443
ISBN 0-8234-0318-1

Thanks to
Kate and John Briggs
and especially to
Margery Cuyler
for having faith in me

Contents

The Case
of the
Missing Six

1 · Quinn O'Hara

Eleven-year-old Damon York wrote the words *How I Spent My Interesting Spring Vacation* on the first page of his spiral notebook. He gazed down at the title, racking his brain to think of an interesting way to begin this blasted English assignment.

"Hang Miss Gray!" murmured Damon to himself, irritably. "Why did I have to get her for a teacher this year?"

He sprawled across the bed thinking, vacation here at Grand-Ada's house? Ha! Rescuing that idiot cat of hers from the highest, puniest branch of the giant elm tree every morning for these past three days is *not* my idea of an interesting vacation. Let me see . . . what else? Well, me and Quinn O'Hara have about finished boarding up the third wall of his tree house at the edge of Spirit Forest. Darn it! I just can't think of a thing to write about for this extra-credit English paper.

Damon York clomped quickly down his grandmother's freshly waxed stairs. He found Mrs. Ada Banner in the kitchen preparing a tasty breakfast for Geraldine, her beloved cat. "Morning, Grand-Ada," Damon said.

The old woman looked at him and smiled. "Why, good morning, child! Do you realize this is the day your mother said she would telephone here? She'll call sometime this morning, so don't you run off anywhere with that little scalawag of an O'Hara boy, now. You hear?"

Damon poured himself a gigantic bowl of cereal.

She continued, "And, I do hope you'll have something promising to tell your mother about the work you've done these past three days on that school assignment, Damon."

"Uh . . . I was up early, writing my spring vacation paper, Grand-Ada," Damon said, heaping sugar on his corn flakes. Well, it's not a complete lie, he reasoned to himself. I have been doing the hard part, the brain work, right?

"And child," his grandmother said, setting a flowered porcelain dish down on the floor for the white cat. "About keeping company with that O'Hara boy . . . you just don't seem to understand that it would pay you to move with the better class of people in life, Damon York! Spending so much of your time with Quinn O'Hara who's been in and out of correctional institutions at a tender age will not uplift you. If only you would try to make friends with the Morrow boy while you're here in Brockton. Joseph Morrow's father and mother are simply lovely people. *So* refined." She sighed, watching Geraldine sniff haughtily at the tuna fish, then stalk away.

Damon didn't reply. This lecture was a familiar one. But, hang around with that fat tub of lard, Joey Morrow? All Joey ever did was sit in his big, fancy house gossiping about everybody in Brockton just like an old woman would. Quinn O'Hara, on the other hand, was all right! Stealing hubcaps and egging a few houses didn't make Quinn a hardened criminal, for gosh sakes! Anyway, most of the trouble he'd gotten into probably wouldn't have happened if his parents had still been around to raise him instead of his tough Uncle Liberty who owned and operated the Liberty Bell Bar and Lounge in downtown Brockton.

Mrs. Banner was still looking expectantly at him, so Damon said, "Grand-Ada, me and Joey Morrow just don't have anything in common. He's twelve, a year older than me. Besides, I haven't even seen Joey since last summer."

"Joey and I," she corrected, lifting her long-haired Persian up onto her lap. "When you glance over your essay for errors, you be sure you've used proper grammar, Damon York. 'Language is the dress of thought and when you speak, your brain is on parade', child."

She stood and looked out the kitchen window. "Well, wouldn't you know? Here comes that O'Hara boy, bright and early! Oh, Damon, after you've eaten breakfast and visited with your company, you will take Geraldine out for a stroll on her leash, won't you? And mind she doesn't slip away from you. She's excitable when she goes out of doors."

Damon went outside carrying his cereal bowl. "Quinn! You want something to eat? I got some corn flakes," he called to the ten-year-old boy parking a battered bike against the elm tree.

The O'Hara boy shook his head. He sat down beside Damon at the redwood picnic table. "Naw, me and Uncle Liberty had us a humongous big breakfast this mornin' about sixish. Daggone, Damon! It's near on to ten o'clock! You just now gettin' up?"

"I had to work on some dumb homework a teacher assigned me this week," Damon said grimly.

"Homework! On spring vacation? You mean to tell me sixth graders in your town got to do homework even when they're not in school?"

"Oh, it's just my English teacher that's like that. And that dadgum Miss Gray, she expects everyone to be William Shakespeare. But, never mind that. What'cha been doing this morning, Quinn?"

"Oh, a little of this, little of that," the O'Hara boy said and reached over to yank off Damon's baseball cap. "You got your ears lowered, Damon York, didn't you? Haw, haw!" Quinn ran his fingers through his own mop of brown hair that hung to his shoulders. "Only way I can persuade my uncle to keep his itchy scissors offa my head is to scrub that puking bathroom in his bar for him ever livelong day. If I don't keep Uncle Liberty happy, he'll either chop off my hair or else dose me good with that confounded bottle of castor oil he keeps so handy."

"Yeah, well, I thought it was worth it to get a haircut just so Grand-Ada would quit nagging about my appearance," Damon said. "She's got some crazy idea kids who have long hair are no-good bums."

"Long-haired bad guys, huh? That's probably why your grandmomma don't have much use for me, Damon."

"No, she's just got outspoken ways, that's all," Damon denied. "Listen, Quinn, where did you get off to yesterday afternoon? I could have used your help getting Grand-Ada's stupid cat down out of the tree again."

"I had me some business to take care of," was the inscrutable reply as Quinn took out his jackknife and began to gouge Mrs. Banner's redwood table.

"Don't carve *my* initials like you did last time, Quinn!" Damon cautioned.

Obligingly, the O'Hara boy turned his attention to whittling a stick. "I never hang around this neighborhood 'lessen you're in town, Damon. Nosirree, your grandmomma sure don't encourage . . ."

"Oh, shut up!" Damon interrupted. "Grand-Ada just worries about, you know, things like me getting ahead in the world. Why, just a while ago, she was trying to talk me into hanging around with Joey Morrow, can you picture it? That nerd!"

There was a pause. Then, to Damon's surprise, Quinn said, "Well, Joey's all right once you get to know him. He's really into cookin', did you know that? He claims he's gonna get into the 'goor-may' restaurant business when he's growed and gets his hands on some of his family's money. Gonna be a famous chef, Joey is."

"These past three days I've been in town you haven't said one word about Joey Morrow, Quinn," Damon said, his mouth full of milk as he drained his bowl. "I didn't even know y'all were friends." He tried to visualize nearsighted, plump Joey Morrow proudly serving up steaming platters of food to scrawny Quinn O'Hara but failed.

"I didn't say we was bosom buddies and all that, Damon! I know you don't care for him. Joey don't exactly think the sun rises and sets on your head, neither."

Damon changed the subject. "Well, getting back to

yesterday. When I called down at the bar, your Uncle Liberty said he hadn't seen you all day. And, he called me David again, Quinn. Sometimes your uncle gets on my nerves, the way he never can call me by my right name."

"He don't mean nothin' by it, Damon. Uncle Liberty's just got rigid ideas about things. Especially dogs."

"Dogs?"

"Nothin'. Go on with what you wanted to tell me."

"Well, I waited yesterday at your tree house for hours, but naturally, since *you* had the nails, I couldn't do any work on that trapdoor. I was bored stiff all afternoon."

"Takes you a hour to tell a thing, Damon, you know it?" Quinn said dryly.

But Damon ignored the sarcastic remark. "I went down to Woods' pet shop and bought me a couple of chameleons, those little lizards that can change their color at will? And I set them on Grand-Ada's braided rug in her parlor. I thought Geraldine was upstairs snoozing her life away on that pink satin pillow of hers, but zap! As soon as I'd set my chameleons down, out tore that stupid cat from behind a chair and sunk her claws in one's tail. Well, I took a swipe at Geraldine to make her let it loose and naturally, Grand-Ada came around the corner just in time to see that. She about had a stroke! I tell you, it's foolish to carry on over a cat like she does. If a person's got to have pets, they ought to keep tropical fish like I do at home in Atlanta."

The O'Hara boy shot a peculiar look at him. "What about carryin' on over a dog, Damon? Don't you think maybe a really special dog might be worth goin' to some trouble over?"

Damon considered the idea but shook his blond head. "No, not really. Why are you so interested in dogs, Quinn? Are you thinking about getting one?"

"Not likely," Quinn replied, looking glum. "Uncle Liberty claims he's allergic to dog hair. Besides, his lot is zoned for business, and he says there's some kind of health laws about us not keepin' dogs inside premises where there's food and drink served or something. But, there oughta be some way . . ." His voice trailed off.

Damon's curiosity was immediately aroused. "Quinn! Did you spy one you liked at the dog pound?"

"Naw, not at the pound. Damon, I . . . uh, did you ever get a look at them purebred show dogs Mr. Sharp raises to sell at his kennel up on route 32? Man, oh man, Sharp's got some of the prettiest Saint Bernard show dogs you ever laid eyes on!"

"Saint Bernards? Those big dogs that carry brandy kegs and rescue lost people in the snow?"

"Well, that business about the Saints totin' brandy kegs is a exaggeration but it's true, they're thought of as workin' dogs," Quinn explained.

"Aren't show dogs expensive?"

"I mean to tell you they are!" Quinn agreed. "Mr. Sharp gets $350 apiece for them pups, sometimes more than that! They all got papers sayin' which full-blooded male dog he bred to which full-blooded female to get the purebred litter. Usually, each and every pup turns out puredee perfect unless . . ."

"Unless? Unless what! How come you're being so mysterious?" Damon prodded. "Are you toying with the idea of buying one of those expensive dogs, Quinn?"

"Naw! I ain't toyin' with nothing!" Quinn snapped. Then he looked around at the Banner house. He lowered his voice. "I already done it, Damon. Listen, you don't breathe a word to a livin' soul now, but . . . I, well, I stole me one of those dogs!"

Damon York stared at the younger boy disbelievingly. Quinn held up his hand. "Wait. Let's us go over there by the honeysuckle bushes, just in case your nosy grandmomma is listenin' somewheres. No offense, Damon."

They walked across the small backyard to the cluster of newly greening vines and bushes that wound over the fence bordering the Banner property. Behind the chain-link fence stretched acres of vast woods, an area called Spirit Forest.

"I been tempted to tell you near about every day

you been visitin' here in Brockton," Quinn began, an embarrassed look creeping over his freckled face. "But, well, heck! I guess I just wasn't absolutely sure what you'd say about me takin' a dog outa Sharp's kennel. Even yesterday, Joey was advisin' me not to mention the business to you, but . . . I decided I need your help. So, I'm tellin'."

"You told Joey what you did, but you didn't want to tell me?" Damon repeated, fighting a twinge of jealousy.

"I stole the pup a longish time ago. About two weeks. Joey helped me build a pen for her deep in the woods, and he went out there regular when I went, until his hay fever come on him. I put a alarm clock and a transistor radio on her blanket to keep her company when I can't be there. But now, I got to figure a new place to hide her. Even in just two weeks the pup's growed like crazy, and she'll dig under that wire fence before long."

"Two weeks! But, how come you . . . what did you do, just spy a dog you liked at that fancy kennel and walk in and take it? How . . ."

"Damon!" called Mrs. Banner from the kitchen window, "your mother's calling you long distance. Hurry, child!"

Damon stood up. "I'll be right back."

"Listen, I've got to go," Quinn said. "Tell you what. Meet me down at my uncle's bar at eleven sharp,

Damon. Don't be late! Then, if you want, I'll show you my pup. But you got to swear on the Bible you'll not tell anybody about her. See you."

Damon went inside the house to talk to his mother on the phone. After he hung up, he reluctantly gave in to his grandmother's coaxing and fastened a pink leash to Geraldine's rhinestoned collar.

"Dratted cat," he muttered as he walked the mewling, nervous Persian up and down the sidewalk. He pondered his friend's tale about the stolen Saint Bernard puppy. Well, Quinn doesn't have to sweat, Damon thought. I won't tell on him but still, taking a valuable dog like that is practically the same as stealing $350 cash or more, isn't it? Quinn could get in real trouble and wind up back in that home for wayward juveniles his uncle had just gotten him out of. He'd better be careful!

After Damon had deposited the white cat safely back in Mrs. Banner's arms, he jogged the mile to downtown Brockton and headed straight for the Liberty Bell Bar on Washington Street. He glanced up at the courthouse clock and saw the time was five minutes before eleven.

Liberty O'Hara, a muscular, balding man looked at him from his spot behind the counter. "The boy ain't here," Liberty told Damon and continued with his job of wiping the large beer steins.

Damon watched a man struggling to win another

free game on the pinball machine for a while, then looked out the window at the clock. Twelve minutes after eleven. Where could Quinn be?

"I told you he ain't here, David!" Mr. O'Hara repeated, scowling. Damon took the hint and went outside to wait.

Now what? he wondered, irritated that Quinn was late. Well, might as well walk down to the pet shop. Wonder if Quinn regrets telling me about the dog? Can't blame him for worrying. His uncle would sure beat the tar out of him if he knew about the dog theft. That tatooed arm of Liberty O'Hara's had settled many a dispute in his bar with just one, powerful jab. Just the same, one of these days I'm going to tell him to his face to quit calling me David, though. Not today, maybe, but one of these days I definitely will.

Damon entered the pet shop and strolled past the small, cluttered counters supporting water-filled tanks of tropical fish.

In a huge tank in the front display window, a snaggle-toothed piranha drifted past Damon's interested gaze. Heck, old worn-out Satan would have a pretty hard time ripping the flesh off anybody's finger, no matter what that warning sign on his aquarium claims!

Damon watched the ugly, flat fish swim sluggishly by, its underslung jaw exposing rows of jagged teeth. Through the watery ripples, he gradually became aware of a face looking in the piranha's tank from the other side. Damon peered, trying to get a better look, but this person's hugely round face was surely distorted in the murky depths of the water. The man was standing outside the store staring in through the plate glass. Suddenly, he raised up so that his face was now above the waterline level. He met Damon's stare squarely, his full, pink lips splitting in a grimace. Ugh! Is that his idea of a smile? marveled Damon, glimpsing a startling display of silvery metal in the man's mouth. Looks like he's got all stainless steel caps on his teeth or something.

Silver glittered in the sunlight as the enormously fat man turned away from the window and entered the pet shop.

Right behind him, Quinn O'Hara came inside, too. Damon gestured toward the white-haired man's broad back. "Who is that, Quinn?" he whispered. "The fattest man in town? I've not seen him in Brockton before."

They stepped back out on the sidewalk and observed the huge man through the window while he made his purchases. Quinn said, "Oh, that's one of the Lemon twins. Name of Olliver. But I do believe this is one of the rare times I seen Ollie here in town. Him and his brother, Osgood Lemon, usually keep pretty much to themselves. They rented a house on the

T.V.A. line last month. But Ossie's as skinny as Ollie is fat, Damon. Just that whitish-blond hair they both got gives a clue about them being twins."

Damon watched the fat Lemon twin point to a metal choke collar and a long chain. Then Ollie picked up something looking much like a huge corkscrew with a handle on one end of it.

"What's that thing he's buying?" Damon wanted to know.

Quinn looked closer. "You ought to know, being a big city boy. That there is a swivel. You stick one end of it in the ground and screw it around good and tight. Then you attach a leash or a rope to the other end where it forms a metal loop. It's for, like, confinin' your dog or cat or even tyin' your horse in your yard so's it could graze in a circle. If you have a swivel, you can get by without a fence. I don't know why Ollie Lemon would be buyin' a swivel. Daggone! He'd have to get hisself a Clydesdale stallion if he was gonna ride a horse!"

"Those looked more like dog supplies to me," commented Damon.

But Quinn O'Hara had lost interest. "Damon, speakin' of dogs, ain't you eager to see mine? Come on, I'll double you 'til the road gets too steepish."

Damon York climbed up on the handlebars and sat facing Quinn. They headed out of Brockton on their way to Spirit Forest, so named by the townspeople years ago because of some silly legend about evil, bloodthirsty goblins that supposedly had once lurked beneath the towering pines.

2 · Mercy Killers

"Gosh almighty, I keep gettin' this terrible pain right smack over my belly button!" Quinn complained, breathing heavily as he dismounted from his bike.

Damon pushed Quinn's bike for him the rest of the way through waist-high weeds. "All right, now tell me the whole story about you stealing this expensive dog from Sharp's kennel," he said and shoved the bike underneath a pile of thick underbrush Quinn had pulled aside.

The O'Hara boy stopped suddenly and clutched at his stomach. Sweat trickled down his face even though the weather was pleasantly cool. "Hold up! Oh, this blasted pain! I musta pulled a muscle or something."

They sat on the spongy ground underneath a weeping willow tree. "Whatever possessed you to break the

27

law and steal somebody's giant show dog, Quinn?"
Damon prompted again.

"She was doomed to die, that's what possessed me,
Damon! Mr. Sharp, he was gonna have all the Saint
Bernard pups in a certain litter put to death by something he called 'mercy killing' but me, I call it pure-
old-dee *murder!*"

Damon was shocked. "Murder! But why?"

"Some folks'll consider doin' anything when there's
money involved. 'Cept for one old man in this town,
he won't! Name of Doc Shaw. 'Course he's got money
a'plenty, maybe that's why. But when Mr. Sharp
called Doc in to ask him would he put the eleven little
bitty pups to sleep, permanent-like, old Doc, he flat-
out refused to give the kennel owner the benefits of
his medical know-how. I heared him say 'twould be a
cryin' shame, and for Mr. Sharp to get somebody else
to do his dirty work for him."

"But, why would this kennel owner want to do away
with eleven of his very own expensive show dogs?"
Damon persisted, confused.

Quinn took a deep breath. "Mr. Sharp owns this
female Saint Bernard named Olga's Sweet Sugar,
okay? And he breeds her every year for champion
pups. This last time she come in season he bred her to
a champion male named Charlie's Masked Bandit, got
that? But, while Olga was still in season, *another* male
dog, a enterprisin' collie named Rags, snuck over

Olga's kennel fence and mated with her, too, that very same week. Mr. Sharp didn't know, though, that Olga had had, you might say, two husbands while she was in heat. He found out about it when Olga's pups was born, 'cause six of them pups looked liked Olga and the Masked Bandit but the other five, they turned up with pointy snouts and stand-uppy collie ears like Rags has. Well, when Mr. Sharp seen what happened to wreck up Olga's money-making litter, he was fit to be tied, he was so mad. Now, do you understand why he was determined to do away with the whole ruined litter, Damon?"

Damon York pondered the tale. "But," he said slowly, trying to imagine a collie named Rags who could actually climb *over* a chain-link fence, "why didn't Mr. Sharp just keep the purebred pups that were fathered by the Masked Bandit and give away the collie-looking pups? I don't really see why . . . "

"I can *see* that you don't see!" Quinn interrupted impatiently. "Look, folks in charge of giving out show dog papers won't register no dog what's come out of a mixed litter, Damon. Some of those Saint Bernard-lookin' pups that you'd think were fathered by the Masked Bandit might still have secret collie blood in them. Olga herself carries the black mask trait even though she don't have one on her own face. Mr. Sharp ain't gonna risk his reputation by sellin' folks pups for a lotta money only to have them come back in a year or two and yell their registered Saint just give birth to a bunch of collie-lookin' pups. That's how come he wanted to do away with Olga's whole troublesome batch."

"So, is the one you stole a valuable show dog, fathered by the Masked Bandit? Or, is it one with secret collie blood, Quinn?"

Quinn shrugged. "How do I know? She sure looks pure. Got the black mask, no collie features that I can spot, but I don't care if she's Rag's pup or the Bandit's pup. All I want to do is keep my pup alive and thumb my nose at the evil idea of euthenasia."

"What the devil's that! Euthenasia?"

"Just a fancy name for mercy killin', like I told you. Didn't you ever hear tell of, oh . . . folks that are real sick and in pain being just allowed to go on and die, Damon? Or maybe somebody giving them a little overdose of sleeping medicine or something to speed things up because the sick folks wanted it that way? Well, that's mercy killin' but the only thing is, it's against the law to do it to humans. Perfectly legal to do it to poor little innocent puppies, though. Laws like that make you want to puke, don't they?" Quinn complained and got to his feet. "Let's us go on. I'm fairly well rested. We got to wallow through some sticker bushes."

They dropped to their knees and crawled through a thick growth of briars and young saplings sprouting in the marshy ground. Quinn swore as he unwrapped a prickly vine from his neck. "That's how it come to me to pick a certain kind of name for my pup. 'Cause of that awful mercy killin' idea. When I slipped in the kennel to grab me a pup the night Mr. Sharp hired a new not-too-bright assistant to work up there, I thought of a good name soon as I had her in my arms, runnin' like a bat outa you-know-where. At the time I was thinkin' that word was spelled y-o-u-t-h-e-n-a-s-i-a, you know? But later, when I looked it up in the dictionary, I found out it wasn't spelled that way a' tall. Didn't make me no nevermind, though. I decided to call my pup Youth on account of the way the mercy killin' word sounded. And, 'cause of her narrow escape from death, too."

"Youth," Damon repeated, pulling cockleburs from his jeans as he inched along. "Well, now that you've told me about everything, I don't see why this Mr. Sharp would care if you stole his Saint Bernard pup or not. I mean, if she's not valuable . . . at least if nobody can *prove* she's valuable, why do you have to keep the pup such a big secret?"

"Damon York, you got a thick head, I mean! I done told you my uncle's said a million times 'No dogs' and he means what he says. Mr. Sharp, if he was so understanding as you seem to think, why didn't he think to give folks in Brockton the pups, huh? Another thing, Sheriff Gates from the county police is just bidin' his time to get something on me so's he can send me back to that juvenile delinquent home. Naw! I promise you I don't want another soul to know I snuck into that kennel and helped myself to one of Olga's Sweet Sugar's pups, valuable or not!"

At last they had made their way to a small clearing. Several yards ahead of them tall pine trees had silently dropped slivered pine needles to the earth. These formed a deep, thick cushion over the ground. The boys walked noiselessly side by side until Quinn stopped. He pointed to a cluster of bushes. "There's her pen. You can't hardly notice it from here, can you?"

When they had gotten closer, Damon heard the sound of a puppy whining eagerly from behind the trembling green shrubs. Inspecting the quivering bushes carefully, he made out the outline of a three-foot-high wire mesh stretched taut from one tree to the next, forming an enclosure. A large pup ran back and forth inside.

Damon saw that Youth did sport what Quinn had described as a "black mask." Her snub muzzle and face were completely black except for one narrow white stripe running between her dark eyes. Her neck and chest were light cream, and the rest of her wriggling body was fawn colored. Damon climbed inside the pen and stroked the happy dog. He was surprised to find Youth's fur felt woolly to the touch, not silky as he supposed her coat would be.

"You're the first person Youth has seen besides me and Joey these past two weeks, Damon. There's not one single house anywhere near Spirit Forest 'cept for the . . . naw, their house is over on the T.V.A. line anyways and that's a goodly distance."

Damon watched his friend fondle the pup's floppy ears. "Whose house, Quinn?"

"Oh, them Lemon twins, remember? Ollie and Ossie? The ones I was tellin' you about when we was at the pet shop? It's not likely either one of them would be pokin' around in the woods in springtime. Not with the snakes out sunnin' and the hornets on the prowl. Just the same, I don't feel good about leavin' Youth here too much longer. You thought of any ideas, Damon?"

Damon tickled the pup's round belly as she lay down between them. Her back leg scratched an invisible itch in the air. "Well, like I said before, stealing this dog is just not as bad as you've been acting like it is, Quinn. Seems to me like you could just keep her as long as you don't go around advertising the fact she came from Mr. Sharp's kennel."

"Damon, you ever set foot inside a detention home?" Quinn demanded, his face taking on the stubborn look Damon knew very well.

"Well, no," Damon admitted.

"Naw! Of course you haven't! But, *I* have! And I ain't got any intentions of ever goin' back in one, not for a little kindly crime such as this. I swear I'll run

away first! Believe me, once you get a bad name with somebody like Sheriff Gates, Damon, a man like that about never gets off your back. My Uncle Liberty sure wouldn't want to be boardin' no stolen dog rightfully belonging to Mr. Sharp. Look! All I wanted you to do was help me think of a good way I could stash Youth somewheres without nobody suspectin' I even got a dog. That's all the ideas I was wantin' from you."

A long silence followed. Finally, Damon said, "Well, I'll only be in Brockton a few days but . . . I'll help you any way I can, Quinn. I give you my solemn promise I will. At least you have a pretty good set-up for the dog until you can . . . until *we* can think of something better."

The O'Hara boy's face smoothed into a pleased grin. He looked down at the fat pup sprawled across his legs. "Okay, little lady, you hear that? Me and Damon York solemnly swear to look out for you the rest of your born days, you good old pup, you!"

When they left, an hour or so later, the boys could hear the Saint Bernard pup yelping sadly, begging to go with them as they made their way back through the woods.

"Did you see how she jiggles that chicken wire fence?" Quinn asked worriedly. "That's why I wished I had me one of them big strong chain-link kennels to keep her in, like Joey Morrow's got for his dog. 'Course it's a laugh, that big old kennel for his tee-ninesy dog.

Joey's got this little animal what looks like a cute brown rat, in my opinion."

"What kind of dog is it?"

"Ummm. Let me think. Mexican Hairless, some folks call that breed. I think Joey says it's some other harder-to-remember name. Chippowah? Anyway, her name's Fifi, and Joey sets great store by his ugly little dog."

They reached the pile of brush and uncovered the rickety bike. Damon noticed Quinn was pressing his hand to his stomach again.

"Damon, you tote me back downtown to my uncle's bar. Then, you can take the bike on home with you," Quinn said and hoisted himself up on the handlebars. "Daggone! With this bellyache I'll not feel like pedalin' around town tomorrow but if I should change my mind, I'll give you a call, okay?"

* * *

That night, Damon lay across his bed in the upstairs bedroom that had once belonged to his mother when she was a girl growing up here in the Banner house. He reread the words he had just written.

MY INTERESTING SPRING VACATION

BY DAMON YORK, SIXTH PERIOD ENGLISH.

In the small town of Brockton, Georgia, there is a very interesting tropical fish section in the local pet shop. In my opinion, fish and chameleons make the very best pets any person could have. At least they are easy to keep safely stashed in one place without the owner having to worry about them breaking down fences or climbing over them, like collies and Saint Bernards do. Also, fish don't rush madly up the tallest tree they can find like some Persian cats like to do. Cities would be cleaner and quieter if people would just be content to keep fish or reptiles for their pets instead of troublemaking dogs and cats.

Damon thought for a minute. Then he wrote: *In a big tank in Brockton's pet shop there is this vicious, bloodthirsty piranha fish named Satan that could probably eat the flesh off a whole cow in six or seven minutes, I'll bet. Keeping a piranha would be educational, too. I could write 800 words easy about a fish like Satan. For instance . . .*

Damon paused. What else was there to say? Tell about how several of old Satan's teeth are missing because he had the dumb habit of biting his aquarium air filter system in half about every other week? Dadgum it!

Disappointed, he stared down into the plastic bucket on the floor by the bed. His chameleons were lying motionless on the sand. He considered putting medicine on the reptile's injured tail but decided against that for fear of burning the delicate skin. Drat Geraldine! thought Damon. As fat as that cat is, anybody can see she certainly gets plenty of food and didn't attack my little lizard for hunger's sake.

"Hey, I got it!" Damon exclaimed loudly, causing the startled chameleon to slither around in fright. The creature promptly turned a creamy, sand color. But Damon didn't notice. He was on his way downstairs to phone Quinn. He checked to make sure Grand-Ada was still sitting out on the screened-in porch chatting with her neighbor before he dialed the number of the Liberty Bell Bar and Lounge.

"He ain't here, David," Mr. O'Hara said. "The boy's gone out in Peterson's truck. He said something about them lookin' for a lost dog."

Damon thanked him and hung up. Lost dog! If Youth had dug under her chicken wire fence . . . no, Quinn would have called me, wouldn't he? He wouldn't have told this Peterson fellow, whoever that is, about the stolen pup. Still, he blabbed to Joey Morrow. Well, too bad I won't be able to tell Quinn about my good idea until tomorrow.

Damon went into the kitchen and eased open the refrigerator door. Grand-Ada had very strict rules against eating late at night, claiming it gave a person ulcers. He jumped at the sound of a loud cry at his feet. The long-haired, white cat had padded noiselessly into the kitchen and was looking interestedly into the refrigerator, too. Hurriedly, he lifted out a pie plate and shut the door quietly. Geraldine gave another piercing wail and hopped up on a kitchen chair, watching him intently. All at once, Damon heard his grandmother's voice call out from the parlor close by. "If you sneak that last slice of my lemon meringue pie, you have to scrub your teeth good, Damon York, you hear?"

Exasperated, he looked over at Grand-Ada's cat as she curled into a fluffy ball. For a moment, it seemed to Damon as if Geraldine had thrown him a mocking smile just before she closed her beautiful blue eyes.

3 · Missing Pets

"Damon, you're absolutely positive you didn't let my Geraldine slip out?" Mrs. Banner asked worriedly for the third time the next morning.

Damon tried very hard not to let his irritation show as he answered, "No ma'am, definitely not! She's probably upstairs snoozing on that little satin pillow you made for her, Grand-Ada."

"No, she's not in the house. I've searched the whole upstairs and down and called and called." Mrs. Banner threw a sweater around her shoulders and stepped out on the front porch. "But, if you're positive you didn't let her slip out the door when you went out for the morning newspaper . . ."

Damon's annoyance rapidly gave way to a feeling of

guilt. Could the sly cat have slipped out the door earlier? It's true the air lock on the front storm door takes a few seconds to swing all of the way shut . . . oh, terrific! Now I'll have to waste all morning helping Grand-Ada snoop around the neighborhood for the stupid, runaway cat!

He joined Mrs. Banner as she went from house to house asking people if they'd seen Geraldine.

"Here, kitty, kitty, kitty, kitty. Oh, Geraldine? Come on, little kitty, kitty!" they called. Damon felt like a fool as he passed by smiling teen-agers standing on the corner washing their cars.

By nine-thirty, Damon saw tears sparkling in his grandmother's eyes as they walked back up her front porch steps. He offered, "I'll hop on Quinn's bike and look all around this area for her, Grand-Ada, okay? Don't worry, we'll find her in a little while."

She nodded and went inside her house. Damon mounted the rickety bike and rode slowly along, wishing sincerely he had stayed in Atlanta this spring vacation.

The loose chain slipped from the sprocket, and he stopped to adjust it as a white van pulled up to the curb close to him. A man called out, "Hey, son! You know where the old mill is at?"

Damon thought. "I believe it's somewhere out on Mud Creek Road, but I'm not sure."

The man made some comment to an unseen companion in the back of the van, nodded at Damon and drove away. In the distance at the bottom of Palmetto Hill, he spied Quinn O'Hara trudging along, so he coasted down, faster and faster, popping a wheelie as he screeched to a halt in front of Quinn.

"You sorry you let me borrow your bike now?" he asked, leaning back to make room for Quinn to hoist himself up on the handlebars.

The O'Hara's boy's face was extremely pale. His freckles stood out against unnaturally white skin. "Naw, I ain't sorry," he told Damon. "I don't care to pedal on account of this pulled stomach muscle I got. Uncle's sure to dose me with castor oil if he suspects I'm feelin' poorly, though. So I let on to him that I was being real generous lettin' you borry the bike. Where you headed?"

"Oh, my grandmother's cat's slipped away again. You want to help me look for a lost pet, Quinn?"

"Ain't that peculiar?" Quinn mused as Damon's legs tiredly pumped the bicycle back up Palmetto Hill. "I was gonna ask you the very same thing."

"You looking for a cat?" Damon York panted.

"Naw, but me and Mr. Peterson rode around town last night tryin' to locate his collie, Rags. Remember the dog I told you about that can climb fences easy as pie? Well, the Petersons left old Rags runnin' loose to guard their house while they went on vacation. They told their next-door neighbor to set out food for him, as per usual when they go off somewheres, but when they come back this time, old Rags, he had disappeared. Even when he's love-sick he don't usually stay gone too long. So, it seems peculiar. Mr. Peterson even give Mr. Sharp a call, but he said he hadn't laid eyes on no mongrel collie. You don't suppose that Mr. Sharp woulda done away with enterprisin' old Rags to get even with him for climbin' over Olga's Sweet Sugar's fence, do you?"

"I don't see how Mr. Sharp could stay in business if he went around killing everybody's dogs, Quinn," Damon said, making a last effort and reaching the top of the hill. He stopped, breathing hard.

"But, you ain't heared it all, Damon. Joey's little Mexican Hairless dog has gone off somewheres, too. Oh, this morning I asked him, and the fancy name for his dog is Chihuahua. Fifi's a Chihuahua, and she's missin' this morning, just like your grandmother's cat."

Damon adjusted the slipped chain again. "That's just a coincidence. Listen, do you want to ride around with me while I look for the cat?"

"I will if you'll haul me. When you get bushed, drop me off at Joey's house. I promised him I'd come up there at lunchtime and sample some of his 'goor-may' cooking. He even said you could come along, Damon. Then after we eat I'm going to Spirit Forest to feed Youth."

"Well, I'll think about it," Damon said reluctantly, not much caring for the idea of having lunch with know-it-all Joey Morrow.

They rode up and down Palmetto Hill while Quinn called out in a ridiculous falsetto, trying to sound like an old lady, "Ooooooh, kittttttttttttttteeeeeeeeeeeee! Here, you kitty, kitty, kitty, kittteeeee!" Damon laughed so hard they nearly crashed into a lamppost.

By twelve-thirty, he wearily agreed to lunch at the Morrow's and pedaled up the long drive leading to Joey's house.

Quinn rang the doorbell, and a voice came promptly over the intercom speaker by the entrance. "O'Hara? Is that you?" Joey's precise voice inquired.

Hearing it, Damon suddenly remembered the Morrow boy's irritating habit of calling everybody by their last name. Fat Joey was a real pain in the . . .

The heavy door opened, and a dark-haired boy wearing thick, horn-rimmed glasses looked solemnly out at them. Damon saw with surprise that Joey had grown much taller since last summer. And, he wasn't pudgy any more, either, Well, well!

"Come in, O'Hara. Hello, York," Joey said unsmilingly and motioned for them to follow him. They passed through several richly decorated rooms. Damon marveled especially at the elaborate chandelier hanging from the ceiling in the dining room over a big banquet table. His eye traveled down the gold-patterned wallpaper and focused on an astounding sight. Mounted on a long, massive support were six fifty-gallon aquariums placed along the length of the room. Eagerly, Damon hurried to admire the various fish drifting in and out of the Canadian pond weed, *Elodea Canadensis.*

"Oh, York, that's right. O'Hara did mention you were interested in tropicals nowadays," Joey said.

Damon nodded, transfixed at the beauty of the huge angelfish in the first aquarium. Look, not one sign of fin rot or Ichthyophthirius, either. Water clear as crystal, good filtering systems here . . . what's that little block wedged in the corner? Oh, yes, Tubifex worms for an all day snack for the angels. Beautiful set-up!

Joey looked thoughtfully around the dining room table. "Will it be okay with you two if we eat in the kitchen? Today's the maid's day off."

Damon had not heard. He said, "Joey, gosh! These angels look terrific! Is this a loach, this funny looking, spotted-eel-type creature with the whiskers? And what kind of scavenger is that?"

Joey glanced in the tank. "Oh, that's a Plecostomus, York. A common member of the catfish family. I'm surprised you didn't recognize that common species. But tell me, do you mind if we eat at the kitchen table?"

Damon tore his eyes away from the third tank of kissing Gouramis. "Eat? Anytime you say, Joey."

"I've spent a lot of time on this meal, and I don't want it to ruin while we stand out here gabbing," Joey said smartly. Quinn followed him through the pantry while Damon gave his grandmother a quick call to tell her where he was, and that he had not yet found Geraldine. In spite of her worry over the cat, he detected a distinct note of pleasure in her voice when she found out he was having lunch with refined Joseph Morrow.

In the Morrow kitchen, Quinn O'Hara sat at a round table while Joey stood at the "work island" in the center of the room. A mouth-watering smell of roasting fowl filled the air as Damon sat down beside Quinn.

Joey Morrow placed two small bowls of some kind of thick, white soup in front of them. Quinn wrinkled his nose distastefully at the soup. "It's cold, Joey," he complained.

"It's *supposed* to be cold, O'Hara!" Joey snapped. "It's vichyssoise, a French recipe. Very nourishing. Try yours, York."

Quinn sipped at his iced tea while Damon spooned the green-flecked, creamy liquid bravely to his mouth. To his mild surprise, he liked it.

"Actually that's just a fancy name for potato soup, York. You probably never heard of it, though, right?" Joey said.

Damon clenched the spoon between his teeth

briefly, irritated since the statement happened to be true.

Quinn said, "Well, anyways, Joey, like I was tellin' you, with your family still not being able to find your little dog, Fifi, and Mr. Peterson still not locatin' his collie, I've had me some hair-raisin' thoughts. You don't suppose some weirdo is runnin' around Brockton collectin' people's pets, do you? And my little pup is all alone out there in the woods . . ."

What an absurd idea, O'Hara!" Joey said, sneering. "Now, listen, I don't even want you to think about going back to Spirit Forest until after you've eaten this nice meal I went to a lot of trouble preparing! I went out and looked for my missing dog all morning and didn't find a trace of where Fifi might have gone. I did call the newspaper and offer a reward for her. Mother's out in the Mercedes right now looking all over town for our Chihuahua but like I told Mother, sometimes dogs and cats just wander off, and that she shouldn't worry so much."

Quinn sipped at his tea, still not tasting his soup. The phone rang and while Joey was in the next room answering it, Quinn said, "Damon, can't you slurp up some of this French goo for me? I sure don't want to hurt Joey's feelings but this is one time his 'goor-may' cookin' don't whet my appetite. Feel my head. Don't it seem like to you I'm hot as a firecracker?"

Damon put his palm on Quinn's forehead. "Yeah,

you're right. You're hot as can be. Maybe you got the flu? When Joey's mother gets back from searching for their little dog, she might can take your temperature, give you an aspirin. After lunch, you can stay here and rest, and I'll run up to the woods and feed Youth for you, okay?"

"She ain't looking for nothin', Joey's mother ain't! Miz Morrow's gone to the beauty parlor just like she always does on a Monday at one o'clock. She ain't sweatin' over Fifi. It's Joey what's worried sick about the little dog, not her." He exchanged his full bowl of vichyssoise for Damon's empty one.

Damon began to eat his second helping. "Quinn, I almost forgot. Last night I thought of a really good idea about what you might be able to do with your pup. You know that kind old man you mentioned? That Doc Shaw? Sometimes old folks will surprise you, Quinn. Might'n he agree to help you out some way with the dog if you tell him point-blank that she's one of the pups you rescued from Mr. Sharp's mercy killing deal?"

Quinn pressed the icy cold glass of tea to his burning forehead. "I don't rightly know what old Doc might say about me stealin' a expensive show dog . . ."

"You don't know for *sure* Youth's a valuable dog! She might just be a Saint Bernard-looking dog with secret collie blood in her, remember? You said yourself that you don't know if Youth's father was really the Masked Bandit or that collie of the Petersons, Quinn," Damon argued.

"Yeah, well, one thing's true, he's got a kind spot in his heart for animals, anyways."

"Who has a kind spot?" Joey wanted to know as he came back into the kitchen.

"Old Doc Shaw, Joey," Quinn informed him. "That old vet who lives way up on Mud Creek Road with that other old geezer who's been workin' for him for about a thousand years, you know? Albert, I think his name is. Damon here was just tellin' me he thought maybe Doc Shaw might be willin' to hide Youth for me or maybe help me out someways."

"Beauregard Shaw isn't a veterinarian, O'Hara," Joey said, opening the oven door. He pulled out a tray containing what looked to Damon York like three tiny roasted turkeys. Immediately, he thought of his sister, Sarah's, pet canary and found himself wondering what-in-the-world-kind of little bird Joey Morrow had cooked!

Joey continued, "As a matter of fact, my grand-mother once told me that Beau Shaw never even finished medical school. He was studying to be a sur-geon, I believe. But, you know how it is. Shaw was the black sheep of his rich family, got into some kind of trouble, squandered a lot of money on this and that . . ."

Joey set the roasted birds on china plates and served his guests. "There! Superb Cornish hens roasted mainly in their own juices, York. Basted with a bit of port wine, seasoned oh-so-lightly with *bouquet garni,* crushed peppercorns, a dash of salt. Actually, fowl prepared this way is not fattening, either," he said with a proud smile.

Quinn abruptly stood, his face flushed. "No offense, but the very thought of food all of a sudden makes me want to upchuck! I'm feelin' sickish, y'all, but it don't have nothin' to do with them baby birds you cooked, Joey, I swear!" The O'Hara boy fled from the room.

Damon inspected the tiny Cornish hen on his plate. Look at the size of those tiny little drumsticks! he marveled. Not much bigger than my finger, for gosh sakes!

He picked up his knife and fork and cut into the roasted bird. He discovered wild rice and chestnut stuffing inside the hen and tasting it, found it delicious. He ate heartily under Joey's approving smile. Soon Quinn returned to the kitchen, his face now white as chalk.

"I'm sick as a dog, y'all," he moaned, splashing cold water on his neck at the sink. "Damon, did you mean it when you said you'd go up to the woods and check on my pup for me? Oh, and wind up the alarm clock, don't forget! She needs to hear the tickin' in the dark, lonesome night."

"By the way, O'Hara," Joey interjected. "These are certainly not 'baby birds' I served. They're full-grown Cornish hens. Not 'baby' *anything!*"

Quinn O'Hara exchanged glances with Damon and nodded agreeably, but when Joey rose to bring more hot Parkerhouse rolls to the table, he shook his head skeptically and made a face.

4 · Goblins in Spirit Forest

After complimenting the Morrow boy on his meal, Damon rode through the streets calling for the cat. He stopped at various houses and asked people but with no result. After hours of fruitless effort, he headed for Spirit Forest. He hid the bike and made the long, uncomfortable crawl through the prickly bushes and vines.

When he arrived at the makeshift pen, he climbed over the low fence to pet the Saint Bernard. He fed Youth and changed her water. Quickly, he checked around the perimeter of the pen to make sure she had not been trying to dig out. Then he sat down, resting his tired legs while the young dog snuggled in his lap, so glad for his company.

Absentmindedly, he looked around at the dense fo-
liage surrounding him. His thoughts turned to a certain conversation he and Quinn had had a few days
ago at the tree house. That day, Damon recalled
Quinn asking, "Damon, you superstitious?" And he
had replied, "Not especially. You mean . . . like thinking if a person breaks a mirror, that would bring seven
years' bad luck? Stuff like that?"

"No, I was thinkin' more about old stories folks tell
. . . Oh, tales about Spirit Forest, for instance."

Damon had stopped hammering on the tree house
door for a moment. "Yeah, I've heard the forest is
supposed to be a bad-luck place."

The O'Hara boy had leaned forward eagerly.
"Smack in the middle of the forest, where the pine
trees grow up almost high enough to touch the sky, is
a certain spot where folks claim goblins creep and
crawl. At midnight, any night of a full moon, these
ugly creatures, *not of this earth,* boil up magic brews
on a open fire and this brew—it's made up of dastardly
things, Damon! Blood and guts and toad's eyeballs,
hairy spider legs . . . and these goblins, they're the
spirits of evil folks dead and gone but restless, don't
you know? Hardly nobody dares to go deep in the
woods to hunt or picnic."

"You don't believe in fairy tales like that, Quinn!"
Damon accused him, smiling.

"Well, there's a grain of truth in everything."

"Goblins dancing? Come on, Quinn!"

"Well, I meant to tell it like it *used* to be. Folks *used* to think the creatures drank the blood and . . ."

"Oh, for gosh sakes!" Damon had said and resumed his hammering. When he had finished, he lifted the lid and fumbled inside the wicker basket his grandmother had given them to use at the tree house. He brought out the jug of water and the sack of sandwiches Mrs. Banner had made for him.

"You callin' me a liar, Damon?" Quinn had demanded angrily.

"No, I just meant that when people get older they don't take superstitious stuff seriously, Quinn. Here, you want a sandwich?"

The O'Hara boy's face had assumed a sly expression. "Well, it's a good thing for me that plenty of folks still do take it serious."

Damon unwrapped a large dill pickle and took a jaw-tingling bite. "What in the heck do you care if folks go poking in those woods or not?"

But Quinn was sinking his teeth into a bacon and tomato double-decker sandwich he'd taken from Mrs. Banner's wicker basket. Shaking his head, he had refused to say another word.

Sitting in those very woods now, Damon understood, days later, why Quinn had been so glad Brockton people were still jumpy about exploring the forest. The reason being, Youth was hidden here, and the chances of her being discovered were not likely, thanks to local superstition.

Oddly comforted by the panting weight of the furry pup stretched across his legs, Damon relaxed and closed his eyes. Come to think of it, maybe it would be pretty nice to have some big old dog for a pet. One that you might even teach to follow a scent to track down criminals; or better yet, locate anybody in the world's missing Persian cat with the greatest of ease.

Without knowing he did, Damon dozed. The sun crept lower down the tree shafts while he and Youth slept. Gradually, he was roused from his sleep by a curious sound. He struggled awake, listening for it again. What was that? He sat up, muscles tense. Youth had raised her head, listening too. Her floppy ears pricked up alertly, and she had stopped panting, her attention focused on some unseen prey.

"There! There it is again!" Damon muttered to himself and got to his feet. The sound echoed through the darkening woods. It began almost like a baby's squalling cry, then faded away into a series of short grunts. Youth whined and looked up at Damon as if for reassurance. Fleetingly, he wondered what a bloodthirsty goblin's call might possibly sound like, but forced himself to dismiss the thought.

His heart beginning to beat a little faster, he bent to give the pup a farewell pat before he climbed over the fence. He scurried through the ancient trees, telling himself the only reason he was in such a hurry was because he needed to hop back on the bike and get in at least another half hour's search for Geraldine before nightfall.

* * *

That night, Damon sat down at the kitchen table to eat the two ham sandwiches his grandmother had made for him. She had gone upstairs with a splitting headache. He glanced over at the empty porcelain dish in the kitchen corner. Geraldine's little bowl, he thought, stricken with remorse. Why, oh why was I so careless about that storm door this morning? Poor Grand-Ada looks terrible but she hasn't said another accusing word to me out loud.

He finished his supper and went into the parlor. His spiral notebook lay on top of the rolltop desk which had once belonged to his grandfather. As he sat down and opened the notebook to a fresh page, thunder rumbled distantly outside. He picked up his pencil and wrote:

RAINING CATS AND DOGS
ON MY SPRING VACATION

BY DAMON YORK, SIXTH PERIOD ENGLISH.

Something strange seemed to be happening in the small town of Brockton, Georgia, during my visit to my grandmother's house. First Rags, a collie who had the ability to scale any fence any man ever built, could not be found by his owners, the Petersons. Then my grandmother's beautiful, white Persian cat vanished without a clue as to how Geraldine got out of the house. Then a boy named Joey Morrow noticed his little brown Chihuahua was gone. Naturally, when these people came to me and asked for my help, I joined in the search for the missing pets. One interesting fact about all this is that some superstitious people in this small town think the missing animal mystery may be connected in some way to the old legend of Spirit Forest. Certain people actually believe goblins and evil spirits gather in the deepest part of these woods on a night of a full moon to cook up some kind of nasty brew made of fresh blood and guts. Not being superstitious my own self, I don't believe the missing pets were collected by some weirdo to be sacrificed by those Spirit Forest goblins. But, it is just an interesting superstition to write 800 words about for this English paper.

Damon hesitated, gripping his pencil. Well, that's not anywhere *near* 800 words, and what else can I say about this mystery? I don't have any idea where the animals are, after all!

"Darn!" he said, resignedly closing his notebook. The clock on the mantle chimed the hour. Eight o'-clock.

Damon looked out the window, seeing the rain

coming steadily down now. Look at that lightning! He counted slowly when he saw the next flare of white light through the parlor window. One . . . two . . . three . . . four . . . there! The clap of thunder. Sounds like the biggest part of the thunderstorm is still about four miles away. Well, Youth's got a shelter to crawl under. She'll keep fairly dry unless the wind's blowing the wrong way really hard. Wonder if all dogs get scared of thunder? And worse, what about the pampered cat? Where would Geraldine hide on such a rainy night? No wonder Grand-Ada had to take a pill for her frazzled nerves. She's probably lying upstairs right this minute picturing her precious Persian's long, white hair all matted and drenched. She's probably imagining the worst about fragile Geraldine not being able to defend herself against some snarling pack of mean dogs.

Damon got up and paced nervously around the room. In a minute, he dialed Quinn's number. "Quinn? I don't have anything to do. My grandmother's gone to bed with a sick headache. She's about to worry herself to death thinking about that stupid cat. She just can't stop her imagination from running wild, thinking about Geraldine out lost in this bad storm."

"I swear, your brain and mine is operatin' on the same wavelength!" Quinn exclaimed. "I been watchin' the lightnin' and worryin' over whether the pup's tar paper roof has give way in all this wet. Listen, tell you what. Uncle Liberty's got a hot game of five-card stud goin' here in the back room with a couple of off-duty cops. Why don't I tell him you called and invited me to spend the night at your place, Damon? Thataway, you and me can take a quick run up to the woods to check on Youth. And, ain't your grand-momma's cat a female? Why, she mighta took to the woods herself. Cats get love-sick worser than dogs."

Hope bloomed in Damon's chest. "You might be right! Just today, I heard some strange cry in the woods, in fact. That could have been a tomcat callin' Geraldine. Well, come on over then . . . but, what about your pain? Is it gone? And will your uncle bring you over, Quinn? I've still got your bike."

"It let up some, I'm proud to say. It's true I got a dab of fever but Uncle don't suspect. I drunk ice water just before he took my temperature a while ago. He did dose me with that evil castor oil, though. Hey, I know what! I'll help myself to Annie Gibson's bike outa her garage next door. Annie won't care. She's all the time scared witless about gettin' her hairdo the tiniest bit outa place so she'll not be ridin' her bike around in this rain."

Damon wrote a note explaining he and Quinn were going out on their bikes to take one more quick look for Geraldine. He taped it on the low-hanging hall light in the downstairs hall where Grand-Ada would be sure to see it if she happened to wake up while he was gone from the house. Then he went to the kitchen and cut slits in two large, plastic trash bags to serve them as rain protectors. He got a flashlight and taped it to his handlebars to serve as a headlight, and was ready when Quinn drove up on a girl's ten-speed, red bicycle.

Soon they were pedaling through the rain, Damon's flashlight shining dimly through the splatters.

When they finally arrived at the edge of the woods, Quinn said, "Damon, the rain's startin' to let up now. Let's us take a different route to the pen so we won't have to wallow through the mud and sticker bushes. It's just a bit longer but we can walk along the swath the T.V.A. line crew cut through the trees. It takes us pretty near where we're aimin' to go."

They walked easily along a cleared trail wide enough for a jeep to travel. Huge metal towers had been erected every hundred yards along the line with heavy electric cables strung between them. The boys passed a dilapidated house. Quinn said, "That's the Lemon twins' place, Damon."

He glanced at it but his mind at that moment had veered back to that afternoon in the woods. "Quinn, what do you suppose that weird sound was that I heard earlier? It sounded like some baby squalling, almost, but . . . it was really strange."

"Coulda been any kind of varmit. Owl, tomcat, raccoon . . . I hear lotsa grunts and groans when I come out here."

They took a narrow trail leading off the T.V.A. line and waded through a pebbly stream. "Watch out for the rusty remains of a old barbed wire fence," Quinn warned.

Now they were walking in waist-high grass. Damon prayed silently that he would not step on a sleeping snake or worse, a wide-awake skunk. He kept his flashlight trained on the marshy ground and stepped exactly where Quinn had walked before him. Gradually, the bushes became thicker and more entangled with vines. Three times Damon stopped to unwrap briars grabbing at his plastic covering. Another time he almost did not recover his tennis shoe from the sucking mud.

All at once they found themselves again in the sweet-smelling grove of pine trees and walked easily on the cushion of pine needles. A soft rustle of evergreen branches whispered far above their heads as the tops of the ancient trees embraced. Brisk winds had sprung up in the steamy damp, and a full moon shimmered beneath fast-moving, lavender clouds.

"Quinn, do you smell smoke?" Damon called softly, immediately recalling the evil legend of Spirit Forest as he glanced up at the full moon.

They stood still. A breeze carried the aroma of charcoal burning and, yes . . . roasting meat? Meat! "Quinn! Didn't you say there weren't any houses close around here?"

"Houses? Naw, 'cept for the Lemon place we passed," Quinn whispered. "Do you catch a glimpse of reddish light over there? Who in creation would be out grillin' a meal this time of night, and right after a heavy rain, too? Let's us ease up and spy."

They crept through the trees and dropped to all fours behind a sparse bit of shrubbery. As they got closer, in spite of his resolve, the dreaded word "goblin" imprinted itself on Damon York's uneasy mind.

A figure was silhouetted against the flickering firelight. The sizzling sound of cooking fat dropping onto hot coals could now be heard clearly. The boys tensed, watching hands reach out to lift a chunk of meat from a skewer resting between two forked sticks. Fascinated, they remained rooted in their uncomfortable positions, knees aching. When the figure finally stood up and faced them, Quinn drew a sharp breath. He gripped Damon's arm and hissed, "That's Ossie!"

The man picked up a bucket of water and poured it over his fire, dousing it thoroughly. Smoke drifted back toward the boys, and Damon squinted his eyes blearily. A sound of metal and glass clinking told them the thin Lemon twin must be loading up his supplies.

After they were satisfied he'd gone, they made their way over to the steaming, wet coals. Damon shone his flashlight down on the remains of Ossie's meal. Small bones were scattered around. Damon knelt and touched something wet and furry. Ugh, what was this? A bloody brown animal skin!

"Quinn, look at this!" Damon said hoarsely. "That man must have killed some animal and skinned it."

Quinn inspected the skin. "Yeah, ain't enough hair on it to tell much. Not a rabbit, though. Just the hide with the head and legs cut off. Could have been a squirrel. Wonder why Ossie's out here at night grillin' his fresh-killed game in all this wet?"

"Ossie is the twin brother of that fat, white-haired guy I saw in the pet shop? Oh, Quinn! I've just had the most horrible suspicion. You know Joey Morrow's little brown Chihuahua is missing? You don't suppose . . ."

In the dappled moonlight, Quinn and Damon squatted down to get a better look at the small, brown animal skin. Did that explain why Ossie Lemon was secretly eating his ghastly meal deep in Spirit Forest? Because he was the one who'd been stealing small animals in Brockton and . . . Damon threw the bloody skin far away from him in disgust.

"Hey, what about Youth?" Quinn exclaimed. "I got to check on my pup!" He leaped to his feet, and

Damon stumbled after him, his brain still reeling with the sickening knowledge they'd just watched a Brockton resident calmly eating roasted dog.

5 · Doc Shaw's Warning

At the pup's pen, Quinn declared, "Damon, I can't help it. I just can't leave Youth all alone here in Spirit Forest now that we know what we know!" He cuddled the happy, drenched dog.

Damon accepted the squirming puppy, grateful for the plastic covering he still wore that protected his chest from Youth's clawing paws. She licked his face as he trudged along behind the O'Hara boy. The fleeting suspicion of what poor Geraldine's fate may have already been made Damon shudder. But, surely that weird Lemon twin wouldn't roast a cat? Anybody that would eat dogmeat . . . Oh, don't think about it and especially don't dare mention this terrible idea to Grand-Ada yet!

"Quinn, let's go on to my grandmother's house. We can sleep out in the garage tonight and keep Youth out there with us until morning. Probably Grand-Ada will sleep like a rock and won't suspect we have the pup with us."

When they reached the bikes, Quinn took off his jacket and wrapped the Saint Bernard in it. He tied the jacket sleeves securely to the handlebars. "Well . . . okay. But before mornin' time we got to figure out a way to tell on bloodthirsty Ossie Lemon without givin' anything away to the law about me stealin' Youth, Damon. Sheriff Gates might stumble on her pen in the woods if he was to go prowlin' around up there to investigate this awful dog-eatin' business. I don't want my name or the pup's brought into this mess. There's gonna be publicity galore, too, I'll wager."

They rode back to Locust Street. Youth whimpered nervously, complaining about her first bike ride. Once they'd gathered sleeping bags and raided Mrs. Banner's refrigerator, they sat in the garage trying to decide what to do with the pup.

"Are you sure your nosy grandmomma's not gonna come out here?" worried Quinn. "No offense, Damon."

"She probably didn't even read that first note I left her, Quinn. It's still on the hall light. Listen, have you thought any more about that idea I had about you asking the kindly old Doc Shaw to help you hide the pup? Another thing, should we go on and call Joey and tell him what Ossie Lemon did to his little dog? It's only ten o'clock, not too late to call. Joey ought to be told . . ."

"Naw, you can't call him and say a thing like that without any bona fide evidence, Damon! With Joey being a cook hisself, he'll really take it to heart! Now that I've had time to think, I'm not so sure that hide belonged to Fifi, anyway. So, let's us hold off on callin' the law on Ossie, one—for lack of evidence, and two —because I got to get the pup safely hidden."

"Okay, then, but let's do something! Go on in Grand-Ada's house right now and give that old guy a call. Ask Doc Shaw point-blank if he'll help with the dog and tell him about Ossie Lemon, too. Get his advice."

"Well . . . I suppose it's worth a try, anyways," Quinn agreed and got to his feet. Damon made himself another peanut butter sandwich and gave one to Youth, too, while Quinn was inside the Banner house telephoning.

When he returned, his freckled face was grinning from ear to ear. "Damon, you was exactly right! Old Doc was wide awake and highly interested, especially in the business about Ossie eatin' folks' pets. He said for us to zip right over and bring the pup. There's just one little snag."

Damon looked at him suspiciously. "Snag?"

A touch of pink colored the O'Hara boy's cheeks as he confessed, "You see . . . uh, I stretched the truth a little . . . what I did was . . . well, when I was talkin' with Doc Shaw, Damon . . ."

"Oh, Quinn, get on with it! What did you do?"

"I give him your name, Damon. I let on to him as if I was *you*, Damon York, callin' to say *Damon York* stole the dog from the kennel, that's what! You know, just in case the sheriff got called into things somehow, then my name wouldn't come into it right at first. You don't care if I pretended to be you, Damon, do you?"

Despairingly, Damon clapped his hand over his eyes. "It's already done, I guess. What's the use of me saying anything now? But, next time, do me a favor, Quinn O'Hara. Ask *my* opinion, first!"

Damon wrote another note to his grandmother. This one said that he'd been invited to stay overnight at Quinn's house and would be back early in the morning. He taped it on the light in the hall, reasoning that if she woke up she wouldn't bother calling the Liberty Bell Bar at eleven or twelve at night to check, would she? No, she'd just fuss tomorrow about him leaving without waking her up to tell her, that's all.

The boys pedaled through the wet streets of Brockton, heading for the road that would lead them to Doc Shaw's place on Mud Creek Road. Youth sat in Quinn's bike basket, seemingly enjoying her ride this time. She held her snub muzzle high in the wind, her liquid brown eyes taking in details of the trip.

When they finally arrived at a run-down mansion, Quinn parked his bike and scooped up his fat pup. He stood beside Damon on the sagging front porch as Damon banged the brass door knocker loudly. All of the windows on the second and third floor of the crumbling brick house were boarded shut. One dim light shone from a downstairs window.

Several minutes passed before the door slowly creaked open, and a red-bearded old man peered out at them. "You the lad that just now telephoned me?" Doc Shaw asked. "Come in. Oh, so there's two of you, eh? Follow me. It's dark in this hallway. Bring the dog. Just put the dog down. It's got legs. Doesn't it have legs? This way, lads . . ."

His wavery voice trailed off as he turned away and limped down a narrow, winding hallway. He led them into what apparently had once been a fine library room when the home was well cared for. Bookshelves from floor to ceiling on every wall were jammed tight with medical books, magazines, encyclopedias, and trophies. A hot plate surrounded by a clutter of dirty dishes stood on a card table in one corner of the room. Against a wall was a daybed covered over with a crumpled maroon and gold wool afghan. On top of this were strewn typewritten pages, a jeweled horse bridle, two currycombs, three tobacco pouches and surprisingly, a bird's nest. Curious, Damon bent to look inside it but found it empty.

"Now then, let's get a look at this pup of Olga's Sweet Sugar, Doc said, settling down in his rocking chair. Quinn brought Youth over to him, and the old man ran his gnarled hands over her head and body. "Let's see . . . good head, occiput moderately developed, skull slightly arched, muzzle doesn't taper, flews curve nicely. Hmmmm. Mouth got a black roof? Black lips and nose, dark eyes—bring it a bit closer, lad— sloping shoulders, deep chest, good straight back. Belly . . . got a fat little belly, doesn't it? Heh, heh! Let's see, does she carry her tail a little too high? Yep, I'd say you got yourself a winnin' bitch out of Olga, lad. Looks like one of the Bandit's offspring, sure as I'm sittin' here. What did you tell me your name was? York, wasn't it?" He looked up at Quinn O'Hara.

Quinn nodded, his expression carefully blank. "Yessir, Damon York, that's me. Definitely."

"Funny, can't think why that name would be familiar to me. We don't have a family of Yorks here in Brockton. Did you just move to town, lad?"

Quinn hesitated, throwing Damon a questioning look. Damon shrugged, irritated by this masquerade. Let Quinn dig his own grave with all this confusion about swapping names!

"Well, I'm visitin' my friend here in Brockton for a while," Quinn said. "We're on spring vacation from school this week."

Doc looked over at Damon. "And this friend, does he have a name?"

Grudgingly, Damon mumbled, "I'm . . . uh, Quinn O'Hara," and cast an exasperated look at Quinn.

The old man leaned back in his chair. He dug in the pocket of his wine-colored smoking jacket and drew out a pipe. "Hand me one of those, lad." He gestured to the pile of bric-a-brac on the daybed. Damon handed him a small, chamois bag. Beauregard Shaw packed his meerschaum with tobacco and glanced down at the young dog who was now stretched out on the rug at his feet. "So, you pulled a slick one on Kenny Sharp, lad, did you? Stole this pup out from under his nose when you found out Olga's litter was doomed? What did Kenny ever do about those other pups, do you know?"

"Naw," Quinn replied, sadly.

"Hmph! Drowned 'em in a rain barrel, more'n likely. I never did have any use for Kenny Sharp nor his father before him. Every one of those Sharps were born hungry to make that almighty dollar. Ken Sharp senior was the same as Kenny, greedy through and through."

"Well, it's a cryin' shame!" Quinn exclaimed, allowing his true feelings to show. "Just because some of Olga's pups wasn't purebred, Mr. Sharp didn't have to be so cruel! He coulda give the innocent pups away to folks in town. He coulda . . ."

The old man interrupted. "Plop yourself down

there on my daybed, lad. I notice you keep holding your belly. You got a stomachache?"

Quinn sat down abruptly. "Naw. But Doc, since you don't have no use for the Sharps, then would you consider lettin' me board my pup here to your place for a while? I could work and pay you for the privilege. I'll buy all Youth's food. Oh, and I'll get a swivel to tie her to so's she could exercise out in your big yard."

"Hold your horses, lad! I understand what you're saying and since you're just visiting your friend here for a time, you'll be taking the dog with you when you leave Brockton, then?"

A long silence followed while Quinn tried to think of a clever way out of the corner he'd talked himself into. Naturally, Doc would jump to the conclusion that he was talking about keeping Youth here for a few days instead of the rest of her life!

Damon watched the old man knit his bushy, red eyebrows. He looked back at Quinn's dismayed face and decided to come to his friend's rescue. "Doc, me and . . . I mean, Damon York and I . . ." Damon began, trying to keep the false identities straight. "Damon and I are kind of in this together even though he is the one who actually stole the dog from the kennel. In case the question ever comes up, *Damon York* did it. Now, uh . . . Damon will be here in town for a long time, and he needs to keep his pup somewhere secretly for a month or two until he can figure out something better. My . . . uh, uncle would be really mad if he knew Damon, my friend, stole this dog. Also, he's allergic to dogs. He can't stand dogs. Did I explain all that pretty clearly?"

The old man puffed on his pipe. "I'm not sure that story is as clear as it might be but if I get the drift, you lads want me to board this stolen dog in secret for at least a month, is that it? Maybe even longer than a month? Hmmm. Let me think . . ."

They waited tensely. At last, he said with a twinkle in his bright eyes, "One time, years ago, I had a run-in with Ken Sharp senior, lads. He wasn't in the dog business. No, he bred show horses, Ken senior did. One time he bribed a judge at the Bluntsville horse show to give first place to his black mare when it should have gone to *my* horse, Lucky Lady. I never did forgive Ken Sharp for that stunt."

Another silence. Then, "Well, I'll tell you what! I'm going to help you, Damon York," he announced to Quinn. "I'm going to let you raise this pup of Olga's and maybe one of these days, oh . . . a year or two from now, lads, we might just waltz her into that kennel and make Kenny Sharp's eyes fall out on his cheeks, might'n we? Heh, heh, heh!"

Quinn gave a great sigh of relief and grinned broadly at Damon.

"Now, let's get on to this other matter," Beauregard Shaw said. "Let's hear this wild tale about Osgood

Lemon secretly dining on roast dog, shall we? And tell it nice and slow so I don't miss any of the important details."

As Quinn began telling him how they'd seen Ossie eating his sickening meal deep in Spirit Forest, Damon noticed Youth had gotten up and was just about to squat over a pile of books on the floor. He jumped up. "Youth, no! I'll take her out Qui . . . Damon."

He picked up the puppy. As he left the room, he heard Quinn declaring his reluctance to involve Sheriff Gates in this pet-killing business unless it was absolutely necessary. But the old man was changing the subject. "You positive your stomach's not hurting you, lad? How come you keep pressing your hand against your belly that way?"

Damon went outside and set the dog down. Suddenly, he was startled by a harsh voice speaking directly behind him. "What you doin' poking around this place?"

A flashlight beamed in Damon's eyes, and he glimpsed an outline of a tall man dressed in a black suit.

"What you doin' out here with this dog?" asked the voice, sounding less threatening.

Damon explained, wondering who the stranger could be. "Me and my friend were invited to come over but just now I had to come out here with the pup so she could . . ."

"Answer nature's call?" the unknown man finished the sentence and laughed heartily. The flashlight clicked off. "I'm Albert. I wasn't expectin' to see some young somebody out strollin' around Beau's front yard this time of night. Sorry if I scared you."

They reentered the house. Albert paused at the library door and nodded a polite greeting to Quinn O'Hara before he spoke to his employer. "I'll say good night, Beau." And he left.

Doc Shaw said sternly, "Well, Damon York, your temperature is 101.8°." He was holding a thermometer up to the light, a disapproving expression on his wrinkled face. "And you say your friend's uncle dosed you with a laxative? Castor oil? Not too bright of this uncle to do a thing like that. You've all the classic symptoms of appendicitis, lad. A ruptured appendix can kill, did you know that? Does this uncle know that?" He turned and stared at Damon. "What's his phone number? I better give him a call."

Alarmed, Quinn O'Hara got to his feet. "Doc, naw! That uncle's . . . he's gone out of town tonight, that's what. Well, he'll be back in an hour or so, Quinn, isn't that right? So, the minute he drives up, we'll just tell him what you said and get him to take me straight to the hospital for a good old checkup. But, for right now, I'm feeling just fine, I swear! Not a pain one! And, we've got to be gettin' along now, so . . ." He edged toward the door. "Thanks a million for lettin' me keep the pup here, okay?"

"Well, you're sure you'll tell this uncle, lad? About what I said?" the old man asked. "And, just wait outside there in the driveway. Albert can tie your bikes on his car and drive you home. You shouldn't be riding a bicycle until after a doctor checks you over thoroughly. In any case, you definitely have an infection somewhere in your body or you wouldn't have that fever."

"Fine," Quinn agreed. "Yessir, you don't need to worry. We'll tell, uh . . . the uncle the minute he gets in tonight." He opened the front door and pulled at Damon's arm.

"One more thing, lad," Beauregard Shaw called down the hallway. "About that roasted dog business? I believe you ought to hold off tellin' folks in Brockton such a tale as that until I've had a chance to talk to Osgood and Olliver myself. I rented that house to them out on the T.V.A. line last month, and I'm of the opinion the Lemon twins are nice enough fellows. It's true one of them does have a problem . . . well, never mind. Just let me talk to them. The main thing for you to worry about, Damon York, is getting yourself checked over by a physician promptly! Good night, lads."

Albert drove them back to the Liberty Bell Bar and Lounge and let them out in front. After he'd gone, Quinn whispered to Damon, "Listen, we got us one more little chore to do this night before I wake Uncle

Liberty out of his sound sleep to ask him to waste his hard-earned money takin' me to some doctor. Damon, now that Youth's stashed at Doc Shaw's, we got to take a quick run back up to the Lemon twins' place!"

"What? Are you crazy? At this time of night? What would be the use?"

"Well, Doc said we needed hard facts, did he not? Daggone! Ain't you been worryin' the Lemon twins mighta et your grandmomma's cat, Damon? Ain't you got no feelin's for Geraldine?"

"But you promised you would see the doctor, Quinn," Damon argued. "You might have that appendix problem Doc Shaw was . . ."

"Well, it's my appendix, and I reckon I ought to be the one in charge of it, not you! I'm going back up to Ossie's for a look-see, and you can just go on home and go to bed, Damon!" Quinn said and got on his bike. Damon stared after him. Dadgum Quinn O'Hara, anyway! he thought angrily. It would serve him right if his appendix swelled up like a ripe tomato and popped, just for being so stubborn.

Knowing perfectly well it was the wrong thing to do, Damon mounted the bike and started after Quinn. He tried not to listen to his conscience telling him he should be letting Mr. O'Hara know that his nephew was riding around Brockton with an appendix that might rupture any second, and doing it to save Grand-Ada's stupid, runaway cat!

6 · The Lemon Twins

"Daggone! Looky what's in the Lemons' garbage can, Damon. I swear this must be poor little Martha's dead body. My, my!" Quinn murmured.

Damon shone his flashlight beam down on a pile of bones and feathers at the bottom of the can. "Whew, it smells awful, Quinn. Martha? Who the devil's that?"

They stared at the decomposed body of a black and white bird. "Damon, Martha's this tame duck what has the run of the neighborhood by the dump. Down by Petersons', you know?"

What makes you so sure this is Martha? It might just be a dead chicken, Quinn."

"When was the last time you seen a chicken with webbed feet? Naw, this is bound to be Martha, and

Ossie musta killed her, too! In fact, just yesterday, now that I think on it, Mrs. Peterson was expression' the worry that Rags mighta got after Martha on a slow day and killed her on account of she liked to quack at him and tease him, like. I forgot about Martha being gone."

"Well, okay, this is hard evidence," Damon said. "We can just take the duck's body back to Doc Shaw, and then he'll believe Ossie is killin' small animals in Brockton."

"We got to get better evidence than this," Quinn argued. "Ossie could just claim he was huntin' and didn't have no idea Martha was tame. No, we got to get Fifi's body or Rags' body or may be your grand-momma's cat, Damon. *That's* hard evidence."

"Okay, let's get it over with," Damon said grimly. "See that side window? Let's spy in there, Quinn."

They crept across the straggling grass in the front yard and came to the shabby house rented by the Lemon twins from Doc Shaw. A crack of light gleamed from a window in back of the house. The boys peered under a shade into a grimy kitchen.

Damon had not really expected to find anyone still awake this late at night but then, he recalled, certain kinds of bloodthirsty creatures stayed up all night long, didn't they?

And sure enough, Ollie Lemon, the hugely fat twin, was awake and sitting at the kitchen table. A bowl was in front of him, and he was sipping a red liquid from it through a glass straw. A dribble oozed out of the corner of his mouth. Red soup . . . red? What kind of soup was red? Tomato soup, sure . . . but that liquid looks awfully *dark* for tomato . . . dark red like . . .

"*Blood!*" Quinn said out loud in a shocked voice. "Ollie's drinkin' a bowl of blood!" he said and slid down the wall of the house, leaning against the fieldstone foundation. He stared up at Damon in the moonlight, horrified.

Fascinated and repelled, Damon could not take his eyes away from the sight. Look . . . there's some dripping out of his mouth. It's running over Ollie's chins. Why does he hold his mouth that peculiar way? Can't he open his mouth? *Whose* blood is Ollie Lemon drinking?

Damon skittered down beside Quinn, unable to watch the revolting sight any longer. "Quinn," he whispered, "you suppose there really are such creatures as vampires? Only maybe the modern-day ones just drink it with straws and bowls, the neat way, instead of grabbing at necks? We'd better get out of here! Wait . . . listen, did you hear that? That's the same weird sound I heard in the woods. Oh, Quinn!"

A screeching bawl echoed through the trees. Another loud cry wailed but was cut short. Agonized howling mingled with a man's voice crying out triumphantly, "Got'cha!"

The boys shrank back against the house as the tall, gaunt form of Ossie Lemon passed by them. He seemed to be struggling with a snarling animal. It yowled and hissed as he thrust its scrabbling body down into a burlap bag. At that moment, Damon understood Ossie had captured some kind of cat. Anxiously, he watched, wondering if it could be Geraldine Ossie was carrying into the house. He peered under the shade, seeing the thin twin enter the kitchen.

"I finally got that tomcat you been askin'. for, Ollie," Ossie said. The fat man at the table nodded, sipping clumsily at his dreadful drink.

"Schlee go shlme good blood in 'em, Oshy?" Ollie asked in a strangely garbled manner.

"What? Good blood? Yep, looks like this tom does have good blood in him. I just hope to goodness you're satisfied now, brother," Ollie said and opened a door leading out of the kitchen. He let a large yellow, striped cat out of the bag, locking the cat inside a pantry.

Damon was limp with relief that it had not been Geraldine, after all.

"Ow! Damon, I feel a real severe cramp comin' on all of a sudden!" Quinn exclaimed, his voice rising with pain. He tried to straighten up to walk. "Let's us get outa here," he begged.

Damon put his arm around him, and they walked toward the T.V.A. line path but Quinn halted, grabbing at his side. He sank to his knees and was in tears when he spoke. "Oh, I can't make it! You was right before. I shoulda gone to the hospital." He clutched at his belly and lay on the grass, moaning. "You got to get Uncle Liberty."

Damon made a split-second decision. Those forboding words of Beauregard Shaw's came back to him. "A ruptured appendix can kill."

Damon broke into a run. There's no time! he thought feverishly, heading straight for the Lemon twins' house. He pounded loudly on the front door. "Ossie! OLLIE! Let me in. Help, HELP!" he shouted, determined to somehow persuade the vampires to let him call the hospital for Quinn's sake.

The front door opened, and Ollie Lemon's astonished round face stared out at him. "Hmph?" Ollie mumbled.

Damon pushed past him, yelling, "The phone! Where's the phone? It's an EMERGENCY!"

Ossie Lemon emerged from the kitchen holding out a telephone. "What's the trouble, boy?" he asked but Damon was dialing O for the operator to tell her to arrange for someone to hurry and come quick to the Lemon twins' house out on the T.V.A. line, that a boy was dying from a ruptured appendix! Then he raced back outside and skidded to a halt beside Quinn O'Hara's doubled-up form on the wet grass. Ollie Lemon waddled out, carrying a blanket and a wet towel.

Damon gently wiped Quinn's face after he vomited violently on the ground. "Quinn, it's okay. The ambulance'll be here any minute. Don't worry," he said over and over, oblivious to the Lemon twins' puzzled stares.

Finally, the ambulance did come screaming over the bumpy trail. The attendants lifted Quinn's body onto a stretcher. Damon got in the back of the vehicle beside his friend. As they raced to the hospital, he reassured the O'Hara boy. "I'll call your uncle when we get there. Is the pain really bad?" He leaned over, gazing into his friend's ashen face but Quinn's eyes were closed. He did not answer.

"He's DEAD!" Damon exclaimed but the attendant sitting on the other side of the stretcher reached out and touched his shoulder.

"No, it's okay, kid. He just fainted."

* * *

Four hours later, Damon finally gave in to his grandmother's pleading and agreed to go home now that Quinn's surgery was over. The doctor who performed the operation clapped Damon on the back and said, "Your little buddy's gonna be just fine, son. We snipped off that red-hot appendix in the nick of time. You did exactly the right thing by calling the ambulance, son." He turned to Mrs. Banner. "This your boy, ma'am? Quick-thinking boy."

She nodded but after the doctor had walked away, she said, "What in the world were you and the O'Hara boy doing way out there on the T.V.A. line in the middle of the night, child?"

Liberty O'Hara happened to come out of Quinn's hospital room at that moment, and he stopped to hear Damon's answer.

"Uh . . . we thought . . . oh, we were looking for your cat, Grand-Ada," Damon said, wondering if he should just go on and tell now about the bloodthirsty Lemon twins. No, wait and tell Doc Shaw about them first. He'd know what to do. "Quinn and I wondered if maybe Geraldine had run off with a yellow tomcat that lives in the woods. That's how come we were at the Lemon place."

The adults seemed satisfied with his explanation but before Mr. O'Hara went back to sit by his nephew's bedside he said, "Thanks, David, the surgeon told me your quick thinkin' saved my boy's life."

Mrs. Banner whispered to Damon after the bar owner turned away, "You boys meant well, Damon, I'm sure, but . . . my Geraldine run off with a tomcat? Never in a million years, child. Never!"

Damon took a last look through the open doorway at his friend who was lying as still and white as a corpse on the bed. The slight movement of an air bubble in the glucose bottle hanging above Quinn's head caught Damon's eye. He stared at the plastic IV tube feeding liquid into the vein in the O'Hara boy's thin wrist and felt quick tears spring to his eyes. He turned away and walked with his grandmother to the parking lot. They rode back to her house in silence, and he went straight upstairs to his bedroom. He threw himself across his bed and fell promptly into an exhausted sleep.

Damon dreamed he was in a strange kind of court of law. He thought he had been called as a witness to testify about the real truth concerning the vampire Lemon twins.

Albert was the stern prosecutor, dressed in black. Damon looked over in the far corner of the courtroom and saw fat Ollie Lemon with his enormous arms wrapped in heavy chains. A trickle of blood dripped steadily from his full lips. Shuddering, Damon turned from the sight and heard the judge pounding a gavel right by his head. Surprised, he looked up and saw the judge was Miss Gray, his English teacher. "I understand you've been working on your spring vacation testimony for this trial, Damon," Miss Gray said and smiled approvingly at him with a mouth that seemed to be filled with some kind of metal. She continued, "But before we hear this witness, Mr. Prosecutor, this court will adjourn for a gourmet lunch at Joseph Morrow's home."

"Hooray!" shouted the jurors.

Pound! Pound! went the gavel again, making Damon's head ache horribly. All at once he found himself in Joey's dining room. He walked over to look in the aquariums. Are those . . . fish? he thought, amazed. He pressed his face to the glass, bewildered at the sight of unusually tiny cats and dogs paddling around contentedly underwater. Oh, there's Geraldine! And . . . could that collie be Rags? Yes, and there is the screeching, yellow-striped tomcat floating by, doing the Australian crawl. Strange. . . .

Damon glanced over his shoulder at the twelve jurors who were locating their proper place cards on the Morrow's banquet table. Joey stood in the doorway, patiently waiting until everyone was seated before he brought in the first course.

"Tubifex worms, everybody," Joey said, smiling. "And Daphnia for the second course, followed by wheat middlings. Sound delicious?"

Damon frowned. Daphnia? Wait a minute! That's dried brine shrimp . . . fish food! He looked closely at the jurors again and realized for the first time that they were giant tropical fish, every one except for the foreman. He was a chameleon, conveniently changeable for the voting's sake. Damon noticed that the Bettas and Danios were muttering something. The guppies look angry, too. Why are they all looking at me? he wondered. Opening and closing those huge mouths . . .

He listened intently and finally did hear a small voice say in his ear, "Child? Damon? Can you wake up now? You've almost slept 'round the clock, child. It's two in the afternoon!" Mrs. Banner said and shook his shoulder gently.

Damon sat up, looking wildly around the room for the angry, accusing jurors. Finally, he realized he'd only been dreaming.

"Grand-Ada, is Quinn still okay? I want to go to the hospital and see him. Do you think they'll allow visitors?" He scrambled to his feet.

"Calm down. I want you to get a refreshing shower and eat a good meal before you go visit your friend, child. And yes, I called just an hour ago. The nurse told me Quinn was doing very nicely. Get washed and come downstairs now, Damon. There's someone waiting to see you in my kitchen," Ada Banner told him with a smile and left his bedroom.

7 · Joey's Lecture

Damon hurried downstairs after his shower. When he went into the kitchen Joey Morrow smiled at him from across the table. "York, guess what? Anne Gibson's mother saw a girl with my Fifi this morning. Isn't that good news?"

"Yeah, Joey, did you get her back?"

"Well, no, Mrs. Gibson caught sight of this girl walking a brown Chihuahua along the sidewalk in front of a supermarket on Highway 58. I telephoned the store manager and told him there would be some money in it for him if he'd call me when he saw the girl go by or maybe shop at his store. So, I consider that good news."

Damon sat down at the table. "Why? You don't even

know if that was your dog, Joey, do you?"

"No, you don't understand! This girl, whoever she is, had tied a string to the Chihuahua's green harness. It's obvious she just took my Fifi home with her. Highway 58 is fairly close to my house. Really, York, it's a big relief to me to know for a fact that O'Hara's crazy idea about some weirdo in Brockton kidnapping people's pets is dead wrong."

Mrs. Banner, standing at the stove, froze. Her spatula was poised over the iron skillet. "What's that you say, Joseph? Someone kidnapping pets in town?"

Joey Morrow looked uncomfortable. "Mrs. Banner, I'm so sorry I said that. I forgot for a moment about your Persian still being missing."

Joey appraised the steaming platter of ham and eggs Damon's grandmother set on the table. "By the way, York, Mrs. Banner was just now telling me how you saved O'Hara's life last night, calling the ambulance in the nick of time. Do you want to go to the hospital to visit him? What happened, exactly?"

Damon covered his eggs with catsup, ignoring Joey's frown. "Yeah, I want to go and see him soon as I eat. I'll tell you all about it later, though, Joey."

"But, I never suspected O'Hara had any trouble with his appendix."

"Joey, I never would have, either! It was Doc Shaw that figured out what Quinn's trouble was. In fact, I should have made him get to the doctor sooner than he did. Doc warned us . . ." Damon stopped, aware that his grandmother had turned away from the oven to stare at him in surprise.

"Why, I never knew you were aquainted with Beau Shaw, child! Anyway, you boys weren't out on Mud Creek Road when the O'Hara boy suffered his attack, were you? I thought you were somewhere on the T.V.A. line."

Damon shoveled food in his mouth, stalling for time. Dadgum it, I talk too much, he thought. He drank several swallows of milk. "Well, Grand-Ada . . . me and Quinn . . . *Quinn* and *I* just happened to chat with Doc Shaw when . . . we were, you know . . . riding around town looking for Geraldine. We stopped and had a little talk with him, that's all."

Joey raised his eyebrows thoughtfully. Would he figure out they'd persuaded the old man to keep the stolen pup? Damon wondered.

"Beau Shaw . . ." Mrs. Banner mused as she set the pan of biscuits down beside Damon's plate. "That rapscallion broke every young girl's heart in Brockton once upon a time." A dreamy look came into Ada Banner's eyes. Then she straightened up abruptly. "Not mine, of course! By the way, Damon, do you want me to drive you and Joseph to the hospital to visit your little friend?"

Damon shook his head. "We can just ride bikes, Grand-Ada. After we check on Quinn, we might look for your cat some more. Okay, Joey?"

The Morrow boy nodded, marveling at the huge amount of jelly Damon was piling on his third biscuit. Damon glanced at him, relieved at least to know that his and Quinn's suspicions last night about Ossie eating poor little Fifi were wrong. If Joey was sure some strange girl had swiped his little dog, well, then . . . could we have been wrong about Ollie being a vampire, too, I wonder? Damon thought. Doc promised to talk to the Lemon twins. Hey, I can go up there maybe and tell him what else we saw through the kitchen window. Tell him about them capturing that tomcat . . . and yes, about that duck's body in the garbage can. No, the best thing would be to not mention any of this to Joey until after I talk to Doc Shaw and Quinn.

Damon stood up. "That was delicious, Grand-Ada," he told the old woman and gave her a quick kiss on her cheek.

She gave him a delighted smile which broadened when Joey said, "And we might go over to my house this evening, Mrs. Banner, if that's all right. Maybe York would like to eat supper at my place."

* * *

At the hospital, Quinn O'Hara lay in his bed, wan and sad. He asked worriedly, "Damon, is the pup still okay? Doc didn't change his mind, did he? And did you tell Joey about his poor little dog? Oh, and . . . about Ollie?"

"Tell me about Fifi?" Joey repeated. "What? York, you didn't . . ."

"No, no," Damon said, turning his head so that he could give Quinn a wink. "Joey, it was a mistake, that's all. At first, we thought . . . uh, we wondered if the Lemon twins out on the T.V.A. line might have seen your dog, but of course, now that you've been told by this Mrs. Gibson that she actually *saw* Fifi this very morning in that supermarket . . ." Here he turned and glared at Quinn warningly. "Well, now we know that most of what we were suspecting last night may not be true, right Quinn? *Right?*"

Quinn hesitated, then nodded, a bewildered expression on his face. He sank back on his pillow, a shadow of a grin beginning to play on his pale lips. "Whew! That surgeon what operated on me come in here this mornin' and laid the law down. When he found out about me fudgin' on the temperature takin' by drinkin' ice water, daggone, he claimed I was flirtin' with death!"

"I tried to tell you . . ." Damon began.

"Damon, *I* know it! Don't lecture me anymore than I've already been lectured. Here, look at this. The doc drawed me a sketch of the little worm-like thing hangin' off my intestine. Well, that's the little dude what got infected somehow and almost busted. He snipped it out, though, he said. And, I get to go home in maybe two days more. Only thing is, I just feel so tired, seems like. Can't seem to stay awake for long at a time . . ."

Damon and Joey sat quietly as Quinn closed his eyes for a moment. Then, he looked dazedly at Damon. "You swear you'll still pretend to be me, Damon, won't you? So's nobody will know Quinn O'Hara stole the pup, just yet? You got to cover for me. You promised . . ."

Damon sighed. "Okay, I will if you want me to, but Quinn, what could possibly happen now? Doc's agreed to keep the pup boarded at his house. He won't care if Damon York stole it or Quinn O'Hara did. The main thing I want to find out when I talk to him is if he's questioned the Lemon twins. I want to tell him about what we . . ." he stopped, realizing Joey's eyes were again looking at him suspiciously.

Damon got up. "You rest now. Me and Joey are going out to look for Fifi and Geraldine. We'll come back for evening visiting hours, Quinn, maybe."

When they were out in the hall, Joey confronted him. "York, what's going on, exactly? What's the big secret about those Lemon twins? Does it concern my Chihuahua or not? After all, I am *twelve,* you know, York! If you and O'Hara have some problem you can't handle, why not tell me? I most certainly would have a better chance of solving it!"

Damon looked at the Morrow boy, the familiar irritation with his know-it-all manner sweeping over him.

"Joey, it's dumb as can be for you to go around calling everybody in Brockton by their last names, you know it? We're not in the Army, you know," he snapped.

Joey's face flushed a deep red, and he turned away. He strode down the hospital corridor without looking back. Damon stared after him, defiantly. His thoughts about Joey were interrupted when a big hand clapped him on the shoulder. He looked up into Liberty Bell O'Hara's rugged face. "Oh, hi, Mr. O'Hara."

"David, I just want to thank you one last time for what you did for my brother's boy," the bar owner said, giving Damon's arm a powerful squeeze.

Damon gathered his courage and said, "Damon."

"Huh?"

"Damon! My name's Damon, not . . . David," Damon said in his politest voice. Did Mr. O'Hara get corrected very often? Probably not!

"Yeah, well, that's a hard name to recollect, boy. You look more like you shoulda been a David to me. Anyways, I just want you to know I ain't never felt as bad as I felt this mornin' when that medical man practically called me a murderer for dosin' my nephew with that laxative one time too many! My poor brother must be twirlin' in his grave if he somehow eavesdropped on the doc scoldin' me. I'd give anything if I could make it up to the boy some way." Mr. O'Hara rubbed his bloodshot eyes with scarred knuckles.

Sympathetically, Damon nodded. Suddenly a bril-

liant plan flashed into his mind. "Anything? You say
. . . you'd do *anything* to make up for . . . uh, not
realizing Quinn had the appendicitis problem? I know
just the thing you could do that would more than
make it up to Quinn. Yessir! And, he'd get well quick,
too, if you did it!" Damon's voice rose with excitement.

"Huh? What'cha talkin' about, boy?"

Damon crossed his fingers behind his back for luck.
"Mr. O'Hara," he said carefully, slowly, "I'm talking
about a . . . *dog!* I happen to know where there's one
he can have absolutely free of charge . . . oh, and it's
a guard dog! One that you could use to protect your
property, you know?"

"Hmmmm. Guard dog for my saloon, you mean,
David?" Liberty asked, his face taking on an interested look. "And, you sure it's free? Them guard dogs
usually cost something."

"No, no! Free as air. Nice, healthy dog. Smart, beautiful, affectionate. You could let her stay outside.
Maybe fence in part of that parking lot beside your
place? Quinn would love to have her."

"I don't rightly know. My daddy always claimed he
was allergic to dogs. I'll have to think on it, David,"
Liberty O'Hara said and clapped him firmly on the
shoulder again. He went into Quinn's room as Damon
smiled hopefully and walked down the corridor. His
heart sang. Maybe? Maybe! If only Mr. O'Hara would

let Quinn keep the pup, one major problem would be solved during this spring vacation in Brockton.

Damon looked around the parking lot for Joey's bike but saw it was gone. Well, the heck with him! I'm heading for Doc Shaw's place now to tell him about my suspicions about Ossie and Ollie. And, if only I could locate Grand-Ada's missing cat, well . . . I could think of myself as the new Sherlock Holmes of Brockton, Georgia, right? Right.

* * *

At half-past-four, Damon was sitting under the lattice-worked gazebo in Beauregard Shaw's backyard. Youth slept contentedly in the afternoon sun, a chewed hambone neatly tucked between her white-ruffled paws.

Doc Shaw puffed on his pipe and adjusted a pillow comfortably in the small of his back as he listened to the end of Damon's story about Ollie Lemon drinking a bowl of blood the previous night. Damon waited eagerly for his reaction.

But the old man merely said, "Well it just so happens I've invited Osgood and Olliver over here for a little chitchat. Matter of fact, I thought I just now heard a car pull in my driveway, lad, did I not? And, it's a good thing you're here, too. We can all sit down and hash out this vampire and animal roasting business for once and for all!"

Damon caught sight of a white Mercedes pulling away from the Shaw house. Joey Morrow stood at the edge of the drive, to Damon's surprise. He hurried to meet him.

"Joey, about what I said, I'm sorry I made you mad . . ." Damon started to say when he got down to the bottom of the sloping lawn.

"Shut your mouth, York!" Joey said furiously. He wiped his tear-filled eyes with his sleeve, holding his glasses in trembling hands. "Oh, yes, I know! I know the terrible secret about Ossie Lemon and what he did to my little dog . . ." His voice broke. "I just now talked to O'Hara. Yes! That supermarket manager called and gave me the name of the girl with the Chihuahua so I talked to her. Sad to say, the little dog wasn't Fifi, after all. So, I went straight back to the hospital, sneaked in O'Hara's room and weaseled the information from him that you've been trying to keep me from finding out. Well, it's too late, York. I even went to the Lemon twins' place but they're not home, so I'm going to talk to this Doc Shaw, and then I'm calling the police to come and arrest those sick, cruel, dastardly . . ."

Joey turned away and began to walk rapidly up the slope, heading for the gazebo where Beauregard Shaw sat, observing them with great interest from his spot in the sun-checkered shade. Damon hurried to catch up with the Morrow boy, warning him, "Joey, we don't have all the facts yet. Be careful what you say, and remember to call me Quinn O'Hara, if you can."

As they ran toward the gazebo, another car pulled up in the drive. A tall, fair-haired man got out, followed by his fat twin brother. Ossie and Ollie walked slowly across the front yard and, as Damon streaked by the house, he was comforted in the knowledge that old stern Albert was probably somewhere in the house and would surely not allow the Lemon twins to cause any harm to come to any boy that might accuse them of eating roasted dogs and cats.

Joey and Damon plopped down on a wrought-iron bench near Doc's rocking chair. The old man looked appraisingly at Joey's tear-streaked face and merely nodded a welcome. He called past them to the twins, "Osgood, Olliver? Come on up here and have a seat, why don't y'all? Albert'll be out here with some refreshments for us in a while. Lord, it's warm for spring, don't y'all think? *I* think it is."

Joey clenched his fists as the men approached. Doc Shaw said cordially, "I don't believe I've had the pleasure of meetin' this new lad, have I, Quinn O'Hara?"

Joey sprang to his feet as the Lemon twins stepped inside the gazebo. "I'm Joseph Morrow, and I'm the owner of the tiny, innocent, trusting, little Chihuahua these two bloodsuckers MURDERED!" he shouted. "And, there's no sense in us all sitting around here pretending to be civilized now that I know that you,

Lemon . . ." Joey pointed his finger at the thin twin.
"Oh, yes, now that I know you're guilty of the most
terrible, dreadful, ghastly . . . you see? I know what
you did! And I'm reporting you to the police after I've
told you to your face what I think of you. York and
O'Hara know. They *saw* you doing it! You'll be ar-
rested. I'll . . ."

"Lad, *lad!* Get ahold of yourself!" interrupted Doc
Shaw. "Quinn, help your friend to compose himself,
why don't you? Now . . ." he turned to the astounded
Lemon twins. "Now, Ossie, Ollie, as you can see, this
dog and cat business is turning into an emotional issue.
I'm just real glad you two could come up here and
straighten it all out. Y'all explain things to this lad. He's
as distraught as can be!"

The old man's calm tone luckily had a good effect on
Joey. He sat down again beside Damon, wiping away
the tears that fogged his glasses.

Fat Ollie's beady eyes grew round with bewilder-
ment in spite of the plump folds of skin surrounding
them. "Whas'e shalking l'about, Oshy?" he mumbled
in an unintelligible slur to his brother.

Ossie Lemon patted his fat twin's arm. "Don't
worry, Ollie. Doc spoke to me on the phone about this
a while ago but I didn't want you to get excited and
get to droolin'. You know how hard it is for you to get
a good breath when you drool."

The thin twin looked speculatively at Joey. "Boy,

Doc told me some boys suspected me and my brother of doin' unspeakable things in Spirit Forest, ain't that right?"

Joey's lip still jutted out stubbornly but he yielded to the pressure of Damon's hand and sat down again.

Ossie glanced at the old man in the rocking chair accusingly. "You, Beau Shaw! You're gettin' a big bang outa this, ain't you?"

Doc Shaw simply puffed another blue cloud of smoke and said nothing. Just then the back door of the Shaw house slammed. Albert walked across the newly greening lawn carrying a tray of glasses. Ice tinkled in a pitcher as the tall man in the black suit came toward the gazebo.

Ossie continued, looking steadfastly at Joey Morrow, "Boy, I'll confess one thing to you and one thing only! I been dreadin' for my brother Ollie to suspect I was sneakin' out in the woods late of a night to roast me some animal over a open fire, that's true. But, now I got no choice. Y'all boys done caught me red-handed!"

Damon and Joey heard those words and goose pimples chilled their flesh. Their worst suspicions were finally confirmed beyond the shadow of a doubt.

8 · Dognappers

Damon York leaned forward, his elbows resting on his knees as he listened, fascinated, to Ossie Lemon's confession.

"You see, boys, I didn't want my poor, hungry brother to smell that tasty meat sizzling, so I been tippy-toein' out every few nights to the woods to cook me up a satisfyin' meal."

"Oh, Oshy!" mumbled Ollie Lemon, a sad look creeping across his roly-poly face.

Ossie continued, "See, my poor twin ain't allowed to eat nothin' on account of he's had to get his teeth wired together. He's livin' on liquids. Show 'em how you can't open your mouth, brother," he instructed his twin, and Ollie obligingly spread his lips so they could see the metal glistening in his mouth. Ollie's mouth seemed to be filled with a double set of wire braces on both upper and lower teeth.

"S'tryin' to loosh s'laighty flounds!" Ollie burbled.

Ossie translated. "Ollie says he's tryin' to loose eighty pounds, boys. When Momma lay on her death-bed last year, she took one last good look at the both of us and give us a terrible scolding just before she up and died. Told us we sure as heck better get ourselves down to a pretty fair-normal size by a certain date or else we wouldn't inherit one thin dime of her money! You might not believe this, boys, but at that time I myself weighed near on to 325 pounds. Yeah, it's true, but I lost all that flab, I'm proud to say. Poor Ollie, he tried his hardest but he just couldn't seem to trim down, no matter what! So, as a last-ditch effort, he agreed to havin' his teeth wired together to keep him from takin' in anything a' tall exceptin' for liquids. Can't y'all see why it would be torture for him to watch me eat a normal meal? That's the whole story!"

"But, what about my dog, Lemon? What about my little Fifi!" demanded Joey.

"Dog? Son, this mornin' when Beau Shaw told me some boys claimed I ate a dog in the woods the other night, I had to think a minute before I could figure out what in the devil . . . Lordamercy! But, here, take a look at this," Ossie said and pulled a rotting head of a dead squirrel out of a paper bag. "That's what I cooked and ate. Not dog. Ewgh!"

Damon said, "Well, okay, we might have made a mistake about Fifi . . . but we saw you capture a tomcat, and we even heard you tell your brother that he had 'good blood' in him. How do you explain that, Ossie Lemon, huh?"

The twins exchanged puzzled glances, then Ossie's brow cleared. "Oh, that old tom? Why, that was a tomcat I brought inside the house to keep company with little Juicy, son. Ollie's female cat, Juicy. That old, raunchy tom's been yowlin' around our place all week wantin' to be sweethearts with her, so Ollie wanted me to just bring him on in and let him and Juicy get together and be done with it. Lordamercy! Did you think we was gonna drink that tomcat's blood?"

Weakly, Damon said, "And that black and white duck we found in your garbage can? Wasn't that Martha? And, Mr. Lemon, wasn't that blood Ollie was drinking in that bowl that night? It sure looked like . . ."

Ollie Lemon clapped his plump hands over his mouth in horror. At that moment, Albert decided to offer refreshments all round. He poured a dark-red liquid from the crystal pitcher, and everyone accepted a glass of the punch except Ollie, who squinched his little eyes shut.

Doc Shaw told them, "Cranberry juice, nice and tart, lads."

Ollie spoke, "Oshy? Sh'aht 'uz sha bowl a borchsh, 'shla betcha!"

Ossie Lemon explained. "My brother says he bets you boys saw him sippin' some beet soup through his straw that night. Beet soup, borscht! Not blood, for Gawd's sake!"

Damon sank back, deflated. "And, the duck?"

"Oh, that duck? Why, I didn't kill that tame little duck! I'm a sportsman, son. What happened to that poor critter was I caught this big stray collie runnin' around in the woods carryin' that duck by its neck. I got it away from him, tried to doctor on it, but it died about fifteen minutes after I'd wrassled it away from the collie."

"A collie?" Joey asked, his interest renewed. "Do you think there could be other dogs up there by the T.V.A. line?"

Ossie frowned. "Nope. Not a one. That's the only dog I seen around there, I swear."

Ollie Lemon made a funny noise in this throat but didn't attempt to say anything.

"That might be the Petersons' collie!" Joey said.

"When did you see the dog last, Mr. Lemon?" Damon wanted to know.

"Whose collie did you say? Peters? No, this dog was picked up by a couple of fellows in a white van. They come by and said it was a runaway. They took the dog on with them."

Damon sipped at his juice. A white van . . . two guys in a van . . . the old mill . . .

"I got it!" he exclaimed, jumping up. "When I was looking for Grand-Ada's cat, these two guys in a van like that pulled up and asked me directions on how to get to the old mill. Dognappers, that's who they are! The guys in the white van."

"Dognappers!" Joey Morrow repeated softly.

The adults and the boys considered this new possibility in the small silence that followed. Albert gathered up the empty glasses.

"Albert, why don't you run the lads down to the old mill in your car after a while?" Doc Shaw suggested as Albert scowled and headed for the house without speaking.

Another long pause. Youth woke up from her nap and stretched. She yawned, showing her sharp milk teeth. Ollie Lemon snapped his pudgy fingers, coaxing her to come to him. "Shchlish is a sline ol puph, Oshy," he said in his garbled way while the puppy sniffed at the squirrel's head.

Damon was too embarrassed to say anything more to the Lemon twins. Gosh, they must think I'm crazy to have accused them of eating dogs and cats! he thought, feeling his face getting red. He glanced at Joey and wondered if he felt the same.

"I suppose a dog of that there breed like you got is worth a humongous amount of money, Beau, ain't it?" Ossie commented. Something in his voice made Damon look up. Am I imagining it or does Ossie sound a little tense? he thought, watching the thin twin's face carefully.

"Yep, if it's a registered dog. Saint Bernards can be costly," the old man said, lighting his pipe again.

"A owner would be terrible upset if something was to happen to a valuable dog like that, Beau, wouldn't you say? Say, have you heard anything about anybody missing a dog like this? Have you, Beau?"

Doc shrugged his frail shoulders. "Don't know as I have. There'd be an ad in the newspaper, I reckon, if somebody had lost a Saint Bernard. Why do you ask?"

"Paper! Me and Ollie don't take the paper on account of all the tempting food advertisements. Same reason we don't watch television. Them commercials get Ollie to droolin' something awful! But . . . you think if somebody was missin' a dog like this one they'd put a ad maybe in the lost and found column, something like that?"

"Sure do. You loose a dog, too, Ossie?"

"No, No! Just forget about it. I believe all this talk about dogs has turned my stomach!" Ossie declared.

Damon instinctively suspected Ossie Lemon was not saying what he really felt. Why was he suddenly so interested in the possibility of some mysterious Saint Bernard being missing? Did he know Quinn had taken this pup from the kennel? Was Ossie hoping to get a reward from Mr. Sharp, maybe?

"Well, Osgood, Olliver," Doc Shaw said, "I appreciate you clearin' this business up for the lads. I knew you wouldn't want folks in Brockton thinkin' you fellows were acting like vampires while y'all were renting that house on the T.V.A. line from me. But, rest easy, I believe the lads are going to be hot on these other fellows' trail starting today. These ones in the van, wasn't it, Quinn?" he looked at Damon with a twinkle in his eyes. "You did say dognappers in a white van, lad, didn't you?"

The Lemon twins stood. Ossie's bony face wore a serious expression as he looked at Damon. "Quinn O'Hara, that your name? Well, Quinn, you boys better not go off half-cocked, accusin' those fellows like you did me and my poor brother! That's my advice to you."

They turned to leave, and Joey impulsively called after them, "Oh, Lemons! It so happens I'm an expert on diet foods. I might be able to help you with the reducing plan, if you like." His tone was apologetic.

Ossie Lemon shook his head but Ollie smiled. He said, "S'lash real nice, Shlowy," before he ponderously waddled after his thin twin.

"That means, 'that's real nice, Joey'," the Morrow boy explained to Damon and Doc.

"*I* can tell what it means, Joey!" Damon snapped, feeling like a fool for accusing the innocent Lemons of any wrongdoing in the first place.

"You lads can go investigate the old mill now. Albert's got the car out in the drive, I see," the old man said, getting to his feet.

They went slowly across the lawn, each boy's mind busy with his own thoughts. In spite of all this talk, I still don't have an inkling as to what happened to Geraldine, Damon thought, disappointedly. The only faint clue we have now is this business about the white van. Well, maybe we're on the right track at last!

They got in Albert's wreck of a car and rode to the old mill in silence. When they arrived, Albert waited in the car for them as they walked around the ruins of what had once been a waterwheel-operated grinding mill for the townspeople of Brockton years ago.

Joey looked at the fallen cypress trees. "Too bad about this property going to rack and ruin. The Bagwells used to own it but I heard they sold it to someone last year."

"There's no sign of dognappers here, Joey," said Damon after they'd inspected the remaining rock wall. The rest of the stone foundation of the mill lay scattered helter-skelter near the bank of Mud Creek. "Let's go on to the hospital and tell Quinn what we know, okay? At least, we know now that the Lemon twins haven't done anything wrong. And, you've got to promise me you won't get so emotional again without any real proof—talking to anyone, like the police, for example, about dognappers in a white van, Joey."

Joey Morrow agreed grudgingly. "I won't tell the police yet, York. I mean . . . Damon," he corrected himself smiling ruefully.

* * *

"Dern it all to heck!" Quinn O'Hara complained as he spooned up the last of his Jell-O. "I *would* have to be stuck up here tonight in the hospital right when there's a bona fide opportunity to catch them dognappers in the white van, Joey!"

Damon said nothing. The way Joey had just told the tale, it sounded as if the men in the van had rounded up Rags and Fifi and Geraldine, and would be caught red-handed any minute! But, what was the sense of arguing? Both he and Quinn were already convinced these men, whoever they might be, were the guilty pet snatchers.

"Liquid diet, my hind foot!" Quinn said, pushing away his tray. "I'd give anything to sink my teeth in some of your good 'goor-may' cookin' as of right this minute, Joey. My appetite's come back with a bang, I mean. Damon ate supper at your place tonight, you say? I bet y'all had something scrumptious!"

"Roast beef rare, O'Hara," Joey said, smiling proudly. "York, I mean, Damon, seemed to enjoy his. Of course, I tossed a little Caesar salad . . ."

"Stop! Don't tell me about it, Joey. You're makin' me hungrier than ever!" Quinn said.

"Your uncle thinks you're getting along really well," Damon said. "You'll probably get a regular breakfast in the morning, maybe."

"Oh, let's don't talk about food! Let's talk about y'all's plan on how to catch the dognappers when you go back tonight to the old mill."

Damon and Joey looked at each other. Go back up there tonight? "Well," Damon said slowly, "I guess we *could* take one more look just to see . . . because of that collie and Fifi. But, I don't think those men have Grand-Ada's cat. No, I just can't think they would go around taking cats."

"Oh, I wish I could go along with y'all," Quinn said.

"Go along where?" asked a deep voice. Liberty O'-Hara stood in the doorway. He came into the room. From out of his pocket, he pulled a large dog collar embedded with brass studs. "Here's something you might be needin', nephew," he said. A shy grin played on the man's roughhewn face as he sat down beside Quinn's bed.

The O'Hara boy fingered the collar. "What'cha mean, Uncle?"

"Well, ain't this here new guard dog David's been tellin' me about gonna need a collar when we bring it home with us?"

Quinn's pale face flushed a deep red with joy. But

he stared past his smiling uncle, looking uncertainly at Damon York. "What'cha been tellin' my Uncle Liberty, Damon?"

"Quinn, I . . . I told him about this really terrific guard dog *I* knew about that would be perfect to protect his property. I suggested to him that maybe he could give you this dog for a pet," Damon explained, carefully.

Quinn's brown eyes turned wonderingly to his uncle. "You mean? Uncle, you gonna let me keep Youth? Daggone! This here is my lucky day, I mean! Joey, ain't this the grandest thing? Daggone!"

Mr. O'Hara leaned over and gave Quinn a burly hug. "You got to get well quick, boy, you hear?" he said, his harsh voice tight with emotion.

Damon and Joey realized it was time for them to leave. As they went out the doorway, they heard Quinn saying, "And Uncle Liberty, wait till you see her! Gonna be a beauty, gonna be a reddish gold with a white ruff around her neck. Big dogs take a longish time to grow to their full size. I hope her coat turns silky like her mother's . . ."

Damon was satisfied. He waited outside the phone booth while Joey called his mother and asked her to pick them up at the hospital. Well, one major problem out of the way, thought Damon. Now, if we would only be lucky enough to somehow find the missing animals, heck, I'd have more than 800 words to put down in my notebook for English. The question is, why in the world would the guys in the white van be going around stealing ordinary pets from people in Brockton, anyway?

9 · Discovery at Mud Creek

"Oh, did you remember to call Ada Banner and make sure it's all right with her if you spend the night here with Joseph?" asked Mrs. Morrow as she turned the car into the curving driveway in front of her house.

"Yes ma'am. I called from the hospital to ask," Damon said.

"And, Joseph, you're determined to go out searching for the Chihuahua again tonight?" she asked her scowling son sitting beside her on the front seat of the Mercedes.

"York and I are going to go out on bikes to ride around, Mother. It's only eight o'clock. At least I can try to look for Fifi. That's better than doing nothing!" He turned dark, angry eyes on his mother.

"Dear, I told you yesterday we can just buy you another little dog! Fifi could be anywhere by now. Run away, picked up by some stranger in a car, run over . . ."

"Another dog? I don't know how you can be so . . . so . . ." Joey jerked open the car door and got out. He ran toward the Morrow garage. Hurriedly, Damon got out, too, leaving a perplexed Mrs. Morrow staring after them.

Quite a difference between her and Grand-Ada, he thought as he ran. Mrs. Morrow doesn't even seem to care at all that the family pet is missing. A person like that just doesn't have any real feelings.

Damon halted for a moment. A person like that? He suddenly recalled that the main emotion he had felt when Geraldine first disappeared was irritation, not genuine worry. Hey, I must have changed a little these past few days, he decided as he joined Joey in the garage.

Joey mounted his black European racing bike and gestured toward a red bike in the corner. "Anne Gibson said you could use her bike, York," he said.

Well, I know these streets like the back of my hand, Damon thought as he and Joey coasted down Palmetto Hill. As he sped recklessly, he wondered if Joey had thought to bring along the rope just in case they did find any missing pets.

They reached Brockton's city streets, and Damon

almost slammed into Joey's bike when he unexpectedly stopped in front of the police station on Jefferson street instead of going straight through town.

"Joey, what?"

"York, I'm going in to talk to the police about these dognappers in the white van."

"You promised me and Quinn you wouldn't!"

"I know, but now that his uncle said he could keep the pup, there's no need for secrecy anymore. We need help, York! We can't capture these guys all by ourselves. Be sensible!" Joey said as he parked his bike and went up the steps leading to the police station.

Damon followed him into a small cluttered room. A heavyset man behind a desk glanced at them.

"What do you boys want?" the man at the desk asked.

"My name is Morrow and this is York," Joey said, "and we desperately need your help, Captain. There's a gang of dognappers in Brockton. They are driving around town in a white van . . ."

"Sergeant! I'm not a captain yet, son," the policeman corrected him with a smile. "Dognappers, you say? You got some proof of that?"

Quickly, Joey explained about the missing animals and told of the two men in the van asking Damon for directions to the old mill. He did not bring the Lemon twins or Quinn O'Hara into the tale.

When he had finished, he looked at the man hopefully. "So, will you help us capture the dognappers?"

The sergeant bit the end off of a cigar. "Well, I'll tell you what. It just so happens another dog owner has been here in the station several times askin' us to keep an eye out for his valuable Saint Bernard show dog that was stolen from his kennel. Ken Sharp's of the same opinion you boys are. Hmmm. But, you say you're lookin' for a collie, a cat, and a little brown dog. Chihuahua? Is that the same as a Mexican Hairless?"

"Uh, Joey!" Damon interrupted. "We better go now. We've told the police *all we know!*" he said, edging toward the door. Oh, brother! So, Mr. Sharp had reported his stolen pup missing, after all! Quinn had been dead right!

He tugged at Joey's jacket sleeve. "Joey!"

The Morrow boy turned toward the door, hesitantly.

"I'll tell my squad cars to watch for this white van, boys," the sergeant said. "Right now, they're on the lookout for some joyriders that stole old Miss Lettie Jones' car, but if we spot anybody with animals like you described, I'll tell you about it. Just check in with me from time to time, okay?"

Out on the street again, they whispered to each other. "Joey! We should never have gotten our names connected with the stolen dog idea. At least, *I* shouldn't have!" Damon said anxiously. "Didn't you just now hear that policeman say Mr. Sharp is trying to recover the stolen pup?"

"York, my dog is still missing! I'm going to the old mill to see if those men are there and now, at least, I can truthfully threaten them with exposure. Tell them the police are on their trail, and that they better hand over the missing animals right away! Fifi's fate means a lot more to me than worrying over whether Quinn O'Hara gets a scolding from his uncle!" Joey declared angrily and rode away.

Damon got on his borrowed bike and followed.

On Mud Creek Road, they passed the Shaw house. Damon saw no lights were burning, not even in the library room that apparently served as the old man's main living quarters. Albert was probably asleep, too.

Ahead of him, Joey screeched his brakes and came to a sudden stop. "York! switch off your headlight!" he whispered hoarsely.

They parked their bikes in the weeds and crept slowly up behind a large pile of rotting lumber. In the dark, Damon watched the moon reflecting unevenly on the shimmering creek. A mournful hoot from a nearby owl in a cypress tree echoed softly across the water. A dog barked.

"York, did you hear? Dogs!" Joey exclaimed quietly.

The direction of the wind changed, and suddenly the sound of men's voices filtered down to them through the trees. The boys moved closer, their tennis shoes squishing in the marshy ground. Startled locusts leaped and buzzed earsplitting complaints as the boys crawled stealthily through the weeping willow fringes that hung from the trees along the creek bank. Damon heard one voice asking, "How many you reckon we ought to get, Russ?"

"Depends," someone said. "Maybe we've got all we dare take, without the sheriff gettin' wind of us. You want to leave or stay the night here?"

"I don't feel much like drivin' tonight. I'm tired! Listen, Russ, how many did you get after I give that old guy named Albert his share?"

"Some. Nothin' to brag about. That Albert, he's a tough old bird, ain't he? I'm glad he ain't cozy with the law, at least. Well, why don't you count up and see how many we got in the van?"

Damon and Joey backed up until they'd gotten safely out of earshot. Damon whispered fearfully, "Joey, did you hear what they said? Oh, gosh, Albert is in on the dognapper's plan! And, to think Quinn delivered Youth right into his hands! Hey, no wonder he went to the old mill with us today. He was keeping an eye on us to be sure we didn't find any clues about the dognappers, Joey. Doc Shaw told him to take us. ... That means he's in on it, too! Joey, we've got to ride straight back to town and tell the police. *Come on!*"

"Not so fast, York!" Joey whispered back. "I can't leave now. Didn't you hear them say they might drive away any minute? Fifi's got to be rescued first. We can't use the Shaw place to call the police now that we know those two old men are in cahoots with the dognappers. You and I are going to march into their campsite right now and demand they release their animal hostages!"

Joey inched back through the weeds and reluctantly, Damon moved closer but stopped behind a clump of bushes. He saw a white van parked beside the one remaining wall of the rock mill. A campfire threw orange, flickering light against the fieldstone.

His pulse pounding, he experienced a strange sensation of having lived this moment before. The smell of a campfire in the woods late at night, spying on someone who captures animals . . . why, this is almost like that night me and Quinn were spying on Ossie.

"Joey!" Damon whispered. "We'd better think some more about this. We might be wrong . . ."

It was too late. Joey Morrow had jumped up. Brandishing his flashlight, he charged into the dognapper's campsite, screaming curses at the top of his voice while Damon watched his twelve-year-old friend in shocked surprise.

The two strangers stood stock-still, staring at the sight of the unknown boy rushing toward them.

"*Whaaaaaaa!*" Joey shrieked. He halted, breathing heavily with excitement as he clung to a sapling by the edge of the creek. "Stop! We've caught you now, you dognappers! My friend over there in the bushes has got a gun trained squarely on you. Raise your hands. Now, just stand there. His gun has real bullets in it because his father is the sheriff. And, a patrol car is on the way!"

Still crouching in the concealing bushes, Damon understood what Joey was trying to do. He enhanced the Morrow boy's desperate lie by giving a loud whoop. *"Hooooooooooo-haaaaaaaaa!"* Damon yelled, letting the men know he was there, hidden in the shrubs just as Joey had said.

"What the . . . ? Dognappers!" one of the men said. "What the devil's wr-wrong w-w-with you, boy?" he stammered.

Both men raised their hands as they looked nervously out into the darkness, trying to catch sight of Damon. "Listen, we got permission from the Shaw fellow what owns this property to be here. Y'all tell the sheriff's boy that for us," said one man.

Joey's voice trembled with emotion. "Maybe Doc Shaw fooled us but now that we know about him and you two, your evil plan is coming to a screeching halt, you hear? Now give me my Chihuahua right now or I promise you my friend will blow both of your heads off!"

"Your chi-wha—what? Son, you and us are talkin' in circles. Dognappers? Me and my buddy here ain't got dogs . . . we got *fish!* That's what we got! It's true we wasn't supposed to be pullin' in these trout the government stocked the creek with yet, but . . . well, that old fellow what works for the man who owns the property, that Albert? He said he'd look the other way if we was to fish the creek."

"You're a liar!" Joey said angrily and strode across the clearing. He jerked open the back doors of the white van and stepped back as a large collie bounded out. "I knew it. Dogs!" Joey exclaimed triumphantly. He bent to peer inside the van. "Fifi? Here, Fifi. Come on, girl!"

Damon marveled to himself, watching the scene. "That's just got to be Rags, the Petersons' collie!" he whispered as he saw the dog run over to the men's campfire and sniff eagerly at a pan of frying fish.

"Where is she? What have you done with my Chihuahua?" Joey demanded after he'd found the van empty except for some large washtubs filled with water.

One of the men said, "That stray collie is the only dog we got, I swear. We're fishermen. We don't steal folks' dogs. Call your buddy down here so's we can set down and confabulate, son."

A bewildered expression came over Joey's face. "Stray collie? But . . . isn't this the Petersons' dog? Isn't this Rags?"

The man called Russ explained. "Petersons? Some white-haired fellow what lives up on a trail cleared by the T.V.A. near some woods give us this dog. He told us it was a stray and to take it on along with us. That's the truth, I swear it on a stack of Bibles!"

"Wait a minute. Let me think . . ." Joey said, uncertainly. He sat down on a nearby tree stump while the men stood there, still holding their hands in the air. Finally, Damon stood up and walked into the clearing, his empty hands reassuring them that he did not have a gun, after all. The men relaxed.

"Whew! Y'all about scared the you-know-what outa us," Russ said and poured himself a shaky cup of coffee. He tossed a few pieces of the cooked fish to the collie.

"You really the sheriff's son?" the younger fisherman wanted to know. Damon shook his head. "Nossir. I'm sorry we threatened y'all but we really did think you two were the dognappers here in Brockton. We even stopped by the police station just before we came out here and told the police to be on the lookout for your van."

Russ, the older man, threw a worried look at his friend. "You thinkin' what I'm thinkin', Hank?"

Hank nodded. "Dadgum if it's not gonna kill my soul to have to toss all them fat trout back in the creek, though."

"Devil take it!" Russ said.

In the long silence that followed, Damon patted the collie and wondered if this was Rags. It must be. So, Ossie Lemon had lied about these two guys saying the collie was their runaway dog? Ossie had deliberately given the Petersons' collie away and then lied about it. But, why?

"Mister," Damon began, looking at the older man. "You said . . . are you sure the man on the T.V.A. line gave you this dog, saying it was a stray? You didn't tell him this was your runaway collie?"

"No, no! The white-haired fellow, he was tryin' to doctor on some other big old hurt dog when we drove up, and he was havin' a time with this collie gettin' in his way. We just wanted to ask the fellow directions to the old mill is all. He asked us right then didn't we want a stray dog so we said, sure, we'd take him along. We got troubles enough fishin' this creek without stealin' dogs, son. You want the collie? Take him and be welcome!"

Hank nodded silently and as Damon tied a rope around Rags' neck, the two fishermen stared glumly into the fire. Damon and Joey stood at the edge of the clearing, not exactly sure what they should say to these men they had so wrongly accused. At last, Damon said, "Uh . . . I'm sorry we spoiled your fishing trip, Mister."

Russ tossed his coffee out into the fire. "And you say the law is lookin' for our van?"

Damon nodded.

"Better start emptying them washtubs, Hank, dad-burn it!" Russ said and turned his back on the boys.

Happy to get away without a scolding, Damon and Joey moved quickly and quietly away.

10 · Geraldine's Secret

An hour later, after depositing Rags at the Petersons' house and accepting the family's grateful thanks, the boys were nearing Palmetto Hill. They stopped under a lamplight at the bottom.

"I think I'll just go on home tonight, Joey," Damon said, "instead of spending the night at your place, if you don't mind."

"Okay, we'll part company here then, York. But, tell me one thing. Why did you tell the Petersons we found their collie tied to a tree in the woods? Why didn't you tell them about those men in the van?"

"What would be the use? Haven't we caused those guys enough trouble already? Besides, Joey, something one of those fishermen said keeps sticking in my mind."

"What? I don't remember anything in particular."

"Oh, it's probably nothing. Tell you what. Let's meet in the morning right here and look some more for Fifi and Geraldine, okay? I want to sleep on this hunch of mine."

Damon pedaled swiftly away before Joey could worm his suspicion out of him. Why tell him that Ossie Lemon was now on the list of suspects again? No sense in getting Joey all stirred up. Heck, he was a wild man when he started thinking people knew anything about his missing Chihuahua!

Inside Mrs. Banner's house, Damon tiptoed into the parlor and to his surprise, found his grandmother sitting at the rolltop desk. He wondered if she'd looked inside the drawer and read any of the many attempts he'd made at writing the English paper.

"Damon? Is anything wrong? I thought you were staying overnight with the Morrow boy."

"Well, I changed my mind, Grand-Ada. We're going to meet in the morning and look for his dog and your cat again. Both of us got pretty tired, I guess. I thought I'd just come on home."

She nodded, apparently satisfied with the explanation. "Well, don't stay up too much later, child. It's eleven o'clock right now. Oh, this splitting headache of mine!" she said as she rose to her feet. She kissed him good night and padded softly up the stairs.

Damon quickly withdrew the spiral notebook from

the drawer. I've got a pretty good idea of what I can write about, at last! he thought and reached for a pencil. He rubbed his aching knees with one hand while he carefully wrote: *Me and my two buddies . . .*

Damon frowned and crossed out the last sentence. He began again: *Well, my two buddies and I have been following one false clue after another concerning this mystery about missing animals in the town of Brockton, Georgia.*

Here Damon paused to think. The trouble with trying to write this paper was that no solutions have been found! Little Fifi is still gone. Geraldine seems to have disappeared from off the face of the earth! Mr. Sharp is looking for the pup that Quinn stole from his kennel. No, the answer to this mystery just *has* to involve Ossie Lemon, Damon decided. Ossie lied to us about how those men in the van got Rags. If he lied once . . .

Damon leaned back in his grandfather's swivel chair, thinking hard. That fisherman said Ossie was trying to doctor on another big dog . . . another hurt dog! Hey, could it possibly be?

"Ossie Lemon is the *answer!*" Damon said aloud. He got up and looked out at the giant elm tree in Mrs. Banner's backyard. "Of course! Oh, I've got to call Quinn in the morning and tell him about what I suspect," he said softly, looking at the spreading branches, wishing he would catch a glimpse of a long-haired, white cat clinging to the highest branch in the moonlight. He sighed deeply. Geraldine did have such a passion for squirreling up to the very tip-top of that tree. And, fat as she is, it's a wonder she could even manage to climb so high.

"Fat?" Damon said aloud, another thunderbolt of a thought striking him.

He raced up the stairs and pounded on his grandmother's bedroom door. "Grand-Ada! Wake up! I'll bet you a million dollars I know where Geraldine is!" he shouted excitedly.

Mrs. Banner threw open her door and stared at him. Hurriedly, he blurted out his brand-new idea while she listened, astonished. Then her wrinkled features smoothed into a delighted smile.

* * *

The next morning, Mrs. Banner served Damon his breakfast in bed. He looked down at the blueberry muffins, scrambled eggs, slices of crisp bacon, and creamy butter-ladened grits. A tall, icy cold glass of orange juice completed the meal.

"Is Geraldine still doin' okay, Grand-Ada?" he asked. One look at her beaming face told him the answer.

"Oh, Damon!" she said and hugged him, almost upsetting the silver tray she'd placed on his bed. "I believe I'd hand you the moon on this silver platter this morning if I could!" she said. "Yes, and after you eat, come down and see her. She's a little the worse for wear, I will say. I've been tryin' to comb the tangles out of her hair now and again but mostly, I've let her rest. The dear thing is completely exhausted."

"Grand-Ada, if Mom and my sister Sarah could have seen you climbing up the ladder to Quinn's tree house last night at midnight . . ." Damon smiled, remembering.

"I'd have climbed Jacob's ladder to Heaven if I had thought Geraldine would be lying there at the top in my old wicker basket with her newborn kitten, child!" she told him and hugged him again. "I'm just so thankful that nice little O'Hara boy built that tree house!"

Damon finished his breakfast, pretty satisfied with himself for putting two and two together last night and figuring out that Geraldine might have gone off somewhere up high to have kittens. And, sure enough, the cat had chosen Quinn O'Hara's tree house, probably staying there because of the comfortable wicker basket with the convenient folding lid that kept out rain. Funny that she only gave birth to just one little yellow-striped kitten, though. Mmmmmm. The yellow tomcat Ossie put in his pantry that night must really get around! Damon thought, buttering his third muffin.

He took the tray downstairs and found his grandmother bending over the wicker basket in the corner of the kitchen. Snuggled on the pink satin pillow were Geraldine and the tiny kitten.

Mrs. Banner said thoughtfully, "You know, Damon, my Geraldine must have a side to her nature that I never suspected. Imagine her getting in the 'family way' like that without me knowing it!"

The phone rang. Damon hurried to answer it.

"It's me," said a high-pitched, anxious voice.

"Quinn? How did you . . . did you get a phone put in your hospital room?"

"Naw, one of them nurses pushed me down the hall in a wheelchair to this here phone booth, Damon. Listen, I got trouble, and you gotta get over to Doc Shaw's place *right away!* Uncle's gone there to get Youth!"

"Well, so what?"

"Damon, Joey done come up here to the hospital just now and confessed what y'all done last night. He told me the sarge said Mr. Sharp's offerin' a reward for information leadin' to the whereabouts of his stolen Saint Bernard pup and dadgum it, I can't reach nobody, not Uncle, not Doc Shaw, not Albert. You got to go up there and make up a lie, I don't care what it is. Just get my dog away from Uncle and that cop he took with him to pick her up. The sarge'll take one look and know she's Sharp's dog. Oh, I *wish* I could get outa this stupid hospital!" Quinn ended on a desperate note.

"Quinn, no, no! I was going to call you in just a minute. We found Grand-Ada's cat last night, and things are turning out okay. Rags is home. And, I've got this new idea about the missing Saint . . ."

"Shut up, Damon! I don't have time to talk. Uncle could be there already! Either you go up to Doc's and try to spirit my pup away from that cop or I swear I'll never speak to you again." Quinn's voice betrayed the fact that he was crying. The line went dead and Damon knew his friend had slammed down the receiver.

Damon told his grandmother he was going to meet Joey Morrow now, but she barely noticed him. As he opened the kitchen door he heard her whispering to her Persian cat, "Oh, Geraldine, that precious kitten of yours. Since we found him in the basket in the wilderness, and, yes, there was a little stream running nearby, we'll call him Moses, Geraldine, dear."

* * *

To Damon's surprise, his legs didn't ache this time as he rode across town to Mud Creek Road. Must be getting muscles I didn't have in Atlanta, he thought, with a wry smile.

He parked Annie Gibson's red bike in the shade of a Magnolia tree and stared with dismay at Mr. O'-Hara's truck already sitting in Doc Shaw's driveway.

"We got gobs of company poundin' on this front door today. Hidy, Quinn," Albert said as he opened the door.

"Albert, I got to talk to Doc privately first thing! Is

there a policeman in the house? Where's Mr. O'-Hara?"

The tall man looked at him through narrowed lids. "You got trouble?"

Damon hesitated. "Not exactly. *I* know there's nothing to worry about but Quinn is worried sick because . . ."

Albert interrupted, his eyes now suspicious slits. "I thought *you* was Quinn."

"Oh, well, I mean to say . . ." Damon fumbled for words.

A heavyset man looked out of a doorway down the hall at him. "Hey, son," said the sergeant that Damon and Joey had talked to at the police station. "Aren't you one of the boys that was worried about the dog-nappers in the white van? Well, you can put your mind at ease. Turned out they were fellows over from Valdosta, Georgia. They were thinkin' about buying a little land here in Brockton to raise some horses on. Isn't that what they told you, Albert? Didn't you say they were talkin' to Doc about horses?"

"Yep, that's what I told you," Albert said, shooting a dagger-like look at Damon York in case he felt like disagreeing. Damon kept his mouth shut about the trout fisherman.

"Cat's got his tongue, I believe," Albert said and gave Damon a little push down the hall to the door leading into the library.

Liberty O'Hara and Doc Shaw were sitting in chairs, staring down at the Saint Bernard pup sprawled at their feet. Mr. O'Hara was saying, "I swear if I'd had any idea this famous *guard* dog wasn't nothin' but a little old baby . . . Hidy, David," he said, looking up.

Beauregard Shaw's bushy red eyebrows shot up as he caught sight of Damon standing in the doorway. "David, huh?" the old man murmured to no one in particular.

Damon nodded, not daring to speak. Well, now Doc will know for sure that I'm not Quinn O'Hara, he thought, sinking into the closest chair. Behind him stood the sergeant, lighting up a fresh cigar.

The policeman said slowly, between puffs, "Saint Bernard, eh, Doc? Ken Sharp raises that breed down at his kennels. Valuable animals, those pedigreed show dogs. She purebred?"

Doc Shaw yawned, taking his time before he answered. "Well, I'll tell you . . ." His bright eyes bored a hole through Damon. "There's some question about that. This dog here is . . . what you might call a . . . yes, that's it. This is a 'mystery dog', Sarge. But, Liberty . . ." He turned to the bar owner. "She'll make Quinn O'Hara a fine dog—gentle, and a conscientious guard dog for your place, as well. I'll be glad to pass her on to you and your nephew. That way, I can rest assured she'll be in good hands. Isn't that right, *David?*" he concluded, looking quizzically at Damon York.

Damon looked down at the rug and nodded, not daring to speak. What a comedy! I've been called every name this week but my right one! And gosh, is the policeman suspicious about the pup? He must be, or else why would he bring up Mr. Sharp's name?

Damon gathered his courage. "Uh, Sarge, you said . . . Mr. Sharp was missing a show dog from his kennel? Reported it stolen?"

The policeman ground out his cigar in an ashtray by Damon's hand. "Yep, full-grown Saint Bernard. Had a funny name . . . something Sugar as I recall."

Damon's chest let out an explosive sigh of relief. So! My hunch about Ossie was dead on the target! he thought, wishing he could talk privately to Doc Shaw immediately.

"Liberty, I hate to rush you but we'd best be takin' the dog on back to your place. I'll sit in the back of the truck with her just like we planned since you claim to be so allergic," said the sergeant.

Liberty nodded. He rose and shook hands with Beauregard Shaw. "I just wish you could be there tomorrow when we bring my nephew home from the hospital, Doc, so's you could see Quinn O'Hara's face when he gets a look at his own bona fide dog! Quinn had to have his appendix out, you know."

"Yes, so I've heard," came Doc's dry comment. Damon gazed steadfastly at the floor as the men

passed by him. Beau Shaw put his feet up on the otto-
man in front of him and leaned back in his rocking
chair. He closed his eyes.

After Damon heard the truck pull away, he moved
over to sit on the floor by the old man's chair.

At last, without looking at him, Beau Shaw inquired,
"We got us more puzzles in Brockton this week than
a mystery dog, it seems. Just exactly who are you, lad?"

Shamefaced, Damon confessed, "My real name is
Damon York, Doc. But, I promise, there's a good, logi-
cal explanation for Quinn and me fooling you about
who we were."

"That so?" came the lazy reply. The old man still
had not opened his eyes. He rocked gently to and fro.
In a moment, he said, "You're Ada's grandson, are you
not? Didn't your mother marry a York, lad?"

Damon was surprised, but before he could speak,
the old man was saying, "Like a bolt out of the blue,
I had suddenly recalled some lad saying something
one day about 'Grand-Ada's missing cat', and it
dawned on me that the poor lad, Damon York, who
was lying up at Mercy Hospital must be Ada Banner's
relative. Only thing was, when I called up to her house
just minutes before you strolled in this very morning,
Ada informed me that no, her grandson, Damon,
wasn't the one who had the emergency operation. It
was highly enlightening to find out from her and Mr.
O'Hara that the *other* lad, that one going by your

name, had the infected appendix. Highly enlightening
. . ." his voice faded.

Damon felt his face getting hot. "Yessir, I imagine
you were really surprised. But, Doc, the reason Quinn
and I lied to you . . ."

"Hold up. Did I ask you why you did it? No, indeed,
I did not! All I asked you was who you were. Enough
said."

Damon drew a deep breath. "Well, do you want to
talk about those guys that lied to you saying they were
looking for property to put some horses on? They
weren't horsemen at all, Doc! They spent all day yesterday up at Mud Creek. And, you own that property,
right? Well, they were fishing . . ."

"Trout. Delicious, too," the old man said with a
smile. "That's enough about that also, lad."

Damon hesitated. "Well, the *real* reason I was want-
ing to talk to you . . . Listen, Doc, the other day, Ossie
Lemon lied to us, to *you* when he told us about the
collie being picked up by the fisher . . . by the horsemen, did you know that? And now, I have reason to
believe that *Ossie Lemon* is the dognapper that stole
Olga's Sweet Sugar from Mr. Sharp's kennel, and he
lied about that, too! You see? Quinn and I were on the
right track, at least, when we thought the Lemon twin
was a suspicious character." Damon looked closely,
wondering if the old man had fallen asleep.

"Poor Osgood. You lads just can't leave that man
alone, can you?" Doc said.

"Oh, Doc, won't you please just telephone him one more time since you two are friends and ask him point-blank if he's keeping Mr. Sharp's show dog somewhere at his place? I think she might be injured, too!"

"No, I won't call him," came the flat reply.

"Then, should *I* ask him? Demand that he give Mr. Sharp back his dog or else?"

Silence.

"Doc, tell me what ought to be done!" begged Damon.

"What ought to be done?" Doc opened his eyes finally and glared at Damon. "This is what ought to be done! You ought to hop on your bicycle and ride on away from here, lad. You've about worn me to a frazzle this week. Ada says you'll be going home tomorrow. Praise the Lord. Maybe then I can get me some rest!" He closed his eyes again.

As if by some mysterious summons, Albert appeared at the library door. "Time for you to be runnin' along, 'mystery boy'," he told Damon in a deep voice filled with repressed amusement.

As they walked to the front door, Damon heard the old man call out to him, "And remind that grandmother of yours to give me a call on the telephone once in awhile. Tell Ada Banner I still remember how she near about broke every young man's heart in Brockton once upon a time!"

11 · Damon's Plan

Damon met Joey Morrow at the bottom of Palmetto Hill after his unsatisfactory talk with Doc Shaw.

"Joey, I've just come from the Shaw place and everything's okay. Mr. O'Hara took the pup home with him. Guess what? You know that Saint Bernard the policeman told us Mr. Sharp was trying to recover? Well, it's not Youth he wants back. Joey, it's Olga's Sweet Sugar that's been stolen!"

"What? Oh, no! I went up to the hospital early and told O'Hara about last night . . ." Joey said.

Damon interrupted. "I know. Quinn called me in a panic. I wish you'd ever learn to keep your mouth shut, Joey. He's all upset for no good reason. In fact, we really ought to call him and let him know Mr.

Sharp didn't talk to the police about the pup, but
. . . oh, heck, we don't have time for that, now! We've
got to get out to the Lemon's place right away. This
is our chance to solve the end of the mystery, Joey."

"The Lemon twins? Do they have Fifi, York? Did
you find out something new this morning?"

"No . . . well, I don't really think they would have
your little dog. But Ossie lied to us about how the
fishermen got Rags, and he sure hasn't volunteered
the fact that he's keeping Olga at his place, so . . . well,
let's go and see, Joey. Let's have a showdown with
Ossie!"

With a hopeful expression on his face, the Morrow
boy pedaled rapidly alongside Damon toward Locust
Street. They took the long route and rode fairly easily
over the cleared T.V.A. line.

When they finally arrived at the Lemon's small,
shabby house, they saw fat Olliver Lemon sitting out
on his front porch cradling a tiny, gray cat. "Schley,
Shloey! Schley Quiynl!" Ollie mumbled through his
wired teeth.

Damon realized the Lemon twins still thought he
was Quinn O'Hara since Doc Shaw had introduced
him to them as Quinn one day under the gazebo. Oh,
well, why bother going through all that explanation
again? The main thing is to confront Ossie with the
fact they knew he had Olga!

"Mornin', boys," Ossie Lemon said, walking out on

the porch. He withdrew a knife from his pocket.

His eyes on the knife, Damon forced himself to say, "Mr. Lemon, I'm just going to say it point-blank to you. I know you stole Mr. Sharp's prizewinning show dog, Olga's Sweet Sugar, and I think you should return his dog right away to save everybody a lot of trouble!"

"I agree, you've got to give Mr. Sharp his dog!" Joey put in.

Damon held his breath. Ossie frowned and dug in his other pocket. He pulled out a large, brown, withered chunk of tobacco and cut off a piece. He inserted the lump of tobacco in his cheek, folded up his jackknife, and sat down on the yellow divan beside his fat twin.

"So . . . the jig is up, eh, Quinn O'Hara?" Ossie said calmly. "You about the curiousest youngster I believe I ever did meet up with. You all the time got your nose in dog business. Ooops! I didn't mean that the way it sounded. Well, all right, boys. You caught me red-handed again, didn't you? I admit it. I got the Saint Bernard back in my woodshed. One thing I got to tell you . . . I shot her!" He held up his hand warningly. "Now, let me finish before you rush off, tattlin' that me and my brothers torture dogs again. Better still, let's us all go 'round to the back, and I'll tell you what happened to the dog."

He got up, and the boys walked with the Lemon twins around the house. Damon and Joey watched as he unlocked the door of a small shed.

"How many dogs do you have in there?" Joey asked eagerly.

Ossie turned and stared at him. *"One* dog! You still didn't find that little brown one you accused me of eatin'? Well, you better not start yammerin' about that again or I promise I'm liable to get hot, boy! *One* dog in this here shed. That's all I got!" He flung open the door.

They looked at the large St. Bernard lying on a bed of cedar shavings. Olga raised her head and looked up at them with dark, droopy eyes. Her heavy tail thumped weakly on the floor when she caught sight of Ossie. She staggered to her feet, and Damon saw a clean bandage wrapped around her back leg. Olga licked Ossie's hand as he stroked her silky, red-gold ears. "There, there girl. Olga? That your name, girl?" Ossie murmured affectionately in a singsong voice.

Damon was thoroughly confused. "What happened? Why in the world did you shoot . . ." he stopped.

"Schlake her l'outside, Oshy," suggested Ollie, making a supreme effort to talk distinctly.

Ossie grasped the collar Olga wore and led her outside to a spot in the shade. He fastened a leash on the collar, and Damon noticed the other end was attached to a firmly embedded swivel in the yard. Dimly, he remembered seeing Ollie Lemon buying a collar and a swivel in the pet shop. So, Ossie had been trying to nurse the dog back to health all this time?

"Now, Quinn O'Hara, don't interrupt me 'til I get done with my story, you hear?" Ossie said firmly. "All right, boys. This is the way it come about that I shot this beautiful dog," he began. "I had took my twenty-two out to hunt in the woods, as per usual. There commenced a rustlin' and a growlin' in the bushes so I sighted my target. The collie that I truly did think was a stray run out at me. I relaxed and lowered my rifle. I'd been seein' that collie from time to time out in the woods and didn't think nothin' about it. But then! Lordamercy, all of a sudden this great big old creature leaped outa them same bushes straight at me, and I swear I thought for just one second that I was being attacked by a big old bear! Well, nobody wants to get clawed and et alive so I fired outa being nervy, without gettin' me a second look. But, the minute I heard the big dog startin' to yelp and howl in pain, I took me a good hard look and realized it wasn't no bear a' tall! No, it was this here poor female Saint Bernard, and she was bleedin' like a stuck pig, poor girl!" Ossie patted the dog's head again, sorrowfully. "She run around and around, yelpin' and carryin' on, and I couldn't get nowheres near her on account of the collie—he turned vicious and began to show his teeth. Just then, lo and behold, the white van pulled up and two fellows wanted to know where the old mill was. Well, it was the perfect opportunity for them to just take the stray collie along with them so's I could get to the injured female and try to doctor on her. They asked me could they help so I told them to take the troublesome collie, and they did. That's the whole story."

"But, why didn't you admit this when we were asking you about the Petersons' collie at Doc Shaw's?" Joey asked.

A touch of pink colored Ossie's bony cheeks. "Well, to tell the absolute truth, youngster, I was feelin' antsy about confessin' to some dog owner that I'd gone and messed up their valuable animal. I'm new in this town, you know. Me and Ollie, we decided we'd try to get the dog healed up somewhat, then, you know . . . oh, so quiet-like, try to find the rightful owner and return the dog in pretty fair shape. You believe me, Quinn, don't you?"

Wearily, Damon sprawled out on the grass. "I just can't believe that I've been running around Brockton all week accusing people over and over again of crimes they didn't commit, Mr. Lemon," he said. "I'm sorry! And Joey here is sorry, I'm sure, that we've bothered you and your brother to death!"

Damon sincerely hoped the Lemon twins would accept his apology and was relieved to see them both smile.

"Thash all l'right, Quiynl," Ollie said, fairly clearly.

"Just the same, Lemon," Joey reminded him, "if you *should* happen to spot a little brown Chihuahua that's wearing a green harness in the woods or on the T.V.A. line, maybe, you will give me a call, won't you? The name is Joseph Morrow, and I have a private phone at my house."

Ossie frowned at the mention of Joey's missing dog again so Damon hurriedly got to his feet. "Let's go and look for her, Joey," he said. "Mr. Lemon's not likely to know anything about Fifi."

The twins waved good-bye to them as the boys walked away through the path leading back toward Locust street. "Joey, let's go to the hospital and relieve Quinn's mind about Sharp's reporting the missing show dog," Damon said. "Then, we can spend the rest of the day trying to track down Fifi. Oh, I almost forgot! Heck, in all this confusion I didn't tell you. We found Geraldine! And, she was in the tree house all this time. Wouldn't it be great if Fifi's disappearance turned out to be something simple like that? Say, Joey, Fifi wouldn't have gone off somewhere to have puppies, would she?"

"Not hardly. I had her spayed last year, York," Joey said. "But, I do hope you're right. I hope Fifi's story has a happy ending like all these other missing pets. Oh, I really hope so!"

* * *

An hour later, the boys had finally filled Quinn O'Hara in on all the facts.

"Daggone! So Olga's Sweet Sugar was really the show dog Mr. Sharp reported missing? And, you mean the sarge actually helped Uncle Liberty carry the pup back to the bar without even knowin' Youth was stolen property? Haw, haw! Why, that makes the cop a ack-sess-o-ry to my crime, then, don't it? Haw, haw!"

All at once his hearty laughter broke off as he caught sight of Liberty O'Hara standing in the doorway to his hospital room.

"What's so funny, nephew?" Mr. O'Hara wanted to know.

"Oh, nothin', Uncle," Quinn replied, grinning.

Liberty sat down beside the hospital bed. "Boy? I got some questions to ask you. You ain't been sneakin' outa this here hospital to run around on the T.V.A. line this mornin', have you?"

"What? Me?" Quinn said, astounded. "Not likely! I took me a ride down the hall in a wheelchair is all. Why, Uncle Liberty?"

"Well, the most peculiar thing . . ." Mr. O'Hara said, his rugged features creased into a puzzled frown. "It so happens I give Ken Sharp a call a while ago to ask him what and how much to feed your new little Saint Bernard pup. Ken Sharp raises this same breed of dog up at his fancy kennel, you know? He was highly interested in your pup, too. Asked all kinds of questions about her. I told him what Doc Shaw said about her being, you know, a 'mystery dog', and that struck Ken as funny, for some reason. And the most peculiar thing of all was your name come into the conversation. Yep, in fact the kennel owner, he said for me to give you his sincere thanks for convincing some fellow on the T.V.A. line to call him up this mornin' to tell him where his prizewinnin' show dog was. Ken Sharp says this fellows says *you*, Quinn O'Hara, were out to his place this mornin' and let him know the dog belonged to Sharp's kennel. Mr. Sharp said to tell you he thought you was a pretty enterprisin' boy, all the way 'round, and that he was so glad to get his Saint Bernard show dog back, he'd be glad to give you any free advice you needed about raisin' your little mystery pup that Doc Shaw give you. So, can you explain what Sharp is talkin' about, Quinn?"

Quinn looked at Damon and grinned. Damon grinned back, knowing that Ossie had still thought he was Quinn O'Hara when he and Joey visited the Lemon place a couple of hours ago. So, Ossie had given *Quinn* the credit for getting Olga back to Ken Sharp, huh? What a comedy of errors!

"Uncle . . ." Quinn began, but dissolved into laughter. When he'd composed himself slightly, he tried again. "Uncle, I promise you I ain't been gallivantin' around Brockton this mornin' but it's so hard to explain . . ." he began to laugh again. Damon and Joey exchanged glances and chuckled. All three boys laughed and laughed, unable to talk. Gasping for breath, Quinn clutched at his side. "Oh, daggone! I'm gonna split my stitches if I don't quit this, I swear! Uncle, please let me explain later, okay?" And he and Damon roared with laughter again.

Mr. O'Hara stared at the boys suspiciously. "Another thing, Ken Sharp did find out his show dog was not stolen, after all. His new assistant finally confessed to him last night that the Saint Bernard female had got loose when he opened her kennel gate to go in and feed her. Some big old collie was in the pen with her, to his surprise, and knocked him flat. That's how come the show dog was to escape in the first place, Ken Sharp said. He was relieved to know there wasn't no dog thieves in Brockton, he said. But I told him, dog thieves in Brockton? I said that was the stupidest idea I ever heard of! Only a fool would think folks would go around stealin' dogs in such a small town as this," Mr. O'Hara concluded.

At this remark, all three boys went into gales of laughter again. He threw up his hands. "Y'all are carryin' on like maniacs!" he grumbled. "Especially you, David!" he said to Damon York, who only nodded in agreement and weakly wiped his streaming eyes.

* * *

After they left the hospital, Damon and Joey agreed to meet again on Palmetto Hill at one o'clock to continue the search for Fifi. Damon ate his favorite lunch, hamburgers and fries, at his grandmother's house and agreed again and again with her that Moses was a perfect name for Geraldine's yellow kitten. The phone rang and Damon answered it.

Joey Morrow's tense voice came over the line. "York . . . Damon . . . Fifi—they found her, the police found her . . ."

Damon could tell Joey was crying. "Joey, is she hurt?"

"No, she's . . . oh, Damon, Fifi's dead! She was run over by those guys that stole Miss Lettie's car. Those dirty, low-down . . . a policeman found her little body on the side of a highway leading out of town. I don't know how in the world she got way out there! Oh, Damon, I can't talk to you anymore right now . . ." Joey hung up, sobbing.

Damon sat down at the rolltop desk. Poor, poor Joey! he thought, sadly. Everybody ended up happy except him, and it's not fair.

His gaze fell on the lines he'd written during lunch. He'd been trying to get at least one page done on his English assignment before meeting the Morrow boy to continue searching for Fifi. Now there was no need to look for the Chihuahua.

Damon had written: *"And I do hope my new buddy,*

Joey Morrow, does not mean it when he says he'll never own another dog if he doesn't find Fifi. Because during this spring vacation of mine, I've learned that if a person raises a pet, that person changes for the better. So what if you have to go to some trouble to take proper care of your animal? It's worth it! In fact, in just one short week my own ideas have changed a lot. I can't describe how, exactly, but it's just something I can feel inside.

Damon thought hard. He looked up the number of Sharp's Dog Kennel and dialed, his mind busy with a daring plan.

"Mr. Sharp?" he said. "My name is Damon York. I thought you ought to know that Quinn O'Hara wasn't the only kid who helped you to get your valuable show dog back. No, Joey Morrow worked hard to persuade Mr. Lemon to return Olga to you, too. Joey deserves a lot of credit, maybe even some kind of reward. I had this idea . . ." Damon began enthusiastically.

* * *

The next morning was a happy and a sad time for Damon. He was relieved that he'd managed to finally write an interesting spring vacation report the night before. It was entitled *Look Before You Leap in Spirit Forest,* and contained 836 words in all.

Damon was delighted that Quinn would be coming home from the hospital this morning but sad in the knowledge he had to leave Brockton at noon.

Walking into the parking lot by the Liberty Bell Bar and Lounge, he spotted Joey Morrow sitting in the shade petting Youth.

"Hey, Joey!" he called, wondering what kind of mood the Morrow boy might be in today. Had he recovered somewhat from the terrible news yesterday about Fifi?

As he got closer, he saw that Joey's eyelids were swollen as if he'd been crying for a long time. He sat down beside him and stroked the Saint Bernard's floppy ears. "Quinn's not here yet, huh?"

Joey shook his head. "York . . . Damon, my mother got the strangest phone call this morning from Mr. Sharp, the kennel owner. He told her to pass along his thanks to me because he'd found out I helped to re-cover Olga. In fact, he made the most astounding offer! Mother said he wanted me to have the pick of Olga's Sweet Sugar's next litter of pups, can you imagine?"

Damon smiled, dazzled by the immediate success of his secret telephoned request yesterday to Mr. Sharp. "Well, that's terrific news, Joey. Saint Bernard pups are worth a lot of money."

Yes, but he told Mother he'd sell us one at half price. She was really pleased by Mr. Sharp's generous offer."

"Sell! Half price? Do you mean he didn't offer to *give* you a pup? Why, that money-grubbing . . ."

Damon was furious. For the kennel owner to *sell* the Morrows one of Olga's pups had not been part of his secret plan at all!

"Well, I told Mother that I'd think about his offer later. Right now, with my poor little Chihuahua's death so fresh on my mind, I just can't . . ." Joey did not finish the sentence but watching him, Damon felt a spark of hope. Maybe Joey would eventually change his mind? Oh, I hope so, he thought. Even if Mrs. Morrow does have to pay half price for a pup.

Just then, Mr. O'Hara's truck pulled up in front of the parking lot. The boys went to open the wide gate, and Quinn's freckled face beamed at them from out of the truck window. He marveled at the new fence as he got out. Damon held the excited dog back so that she would not jump up on Quinn. He would still be weak for a few days until his appendix incision had healed.

"Daggone, Damon!" Quinn exclaimed. "Youth's growed in just these few days, you know that? I can tell she's fatter, too."

"Get on in the back room of my saloon now, nephew," Mr. O'Hara warned. "You know the doctor said you had to take it easy for a few days. There'll be time enough for you to mess around with your dog, by and by. Go inside and chat with David and Joe, why don't you?"

They all went inside the part of the building that

served the O'Haras as living quarters in the back of the Liberty Bell Bar. Quinn obediently stretched out on the couch while his uncle adjusted his pillows. Mr. O'Hara went back outside to bring in Quinn's suitcase, and the boys watched through the open window as he stopped and patted the puppy.

"Looks like Uncle's done got over his fears of bein' allergic," Quinn commented with surprise. He looked at Joey. "Damon come to see me at the hospital last night and told me about your little Mexican Hairless gettin' run over by them murderin' joyriders, Joey," he said. "I'm just as sorry as I can be that poor Fifi met with a bad end. It makes me feel kinda guilty to see my worries about *my* pup come to a happy end while your . . ."

"I don't want to talk about her, O'Hara, I mean, Quinn," Joey said. The boys sat silently for a moment. Then, hesitantly, Joey said, "Uh, there is a chance . . . well, this morning my mother was trying to persuade me to take advantage of a certain offer Mr. Sharp made us. Oh, well, I'll have to think about that. Listen, Quinn, I've got to go. I'll call you later and ask your advice about something, okay? And . . ." He looked steadily at Damon. "I guess I'll say good-bye to you, Damon. Something just occurred to me . . . There's only one way Mr. Sharp could have possibly known I was involved yesterday in that confrontation with Ossie Lemon about Olga. Thanks, Damon.

Thanks a lot," Joey said solemnly as he opened the door.

After he'd gone, Quinn asked, "Damon, what's goin' on? Shoot! I been stuck in the hospital too long. I couldn't make heads or tails outa what Joey was talkin' about!"

Damon merely smiled and shrugged. "He'll tell you later, Quinn."

"Well, all I can say is, it's a good thing for us, especially Youth, that you come to Brockton this spring vacation, Damon. I mean it!" Quinn declared.

The boys grinned at each other, then gazed out the window at the contented young mystery dog snoozing in the April sunshine.